SHADOWS

of Olive Trees

On Susanne:

A tremendously passionate writer, ... Gervay writes from the heart. Spectrum Sydney Morning Herald

Susanne is one of Australia's most respected authors, writing about issues affecting women and children. Sunday Telegraph

On Butterflies:

Curl up on the lounge, ignore the phone and enjoy. Cosmopolitan Magazine

Compelling? Moving? Inspirational? You're not even close. ... its gift of strength and hope will stay with the reader, long after the book is put down. REACT ACT

On The Cave:

Susanne Gervay's novel is deceptively moving and powerful, all the characters richly drawn and her description of camp life so realistic you feel you are living it. Good Reading Magazine

The sensational new book, The Cave is a compelling, confronting and important book that examines what it means to be young and male in the 21st Century. Queensland Booksellers

On That's Why I Wrote This Song :

This book has fantastic energy to it. Spectrum, Sydney Morning Herald

SUSANNE GERVAY

SHADOWS

of Olive Trees

FLYING ELEPHANT MEDIA

Other Titles by Susanne Gervay:

Butterflies
The Cave
That's Why I Wrote This Song
Next Stop the Moon

Children's Books
I am Jack
Super Jack
Always Jack
Being Jack
Daisy Sunshine
Elephants Have Wings
Boy in the Big Blue Glasses
Ships in the Field
Gracie and Josh

Dedication

Shadows of the past intertwine into the present
creating the future.
To three shadows who have travelled with me – Moya
Simons, Dianne Bates and Joy Dodds.

Published in Australia in 2019
by **Flying Elephant Media**
ABN 74 622 785 264

FE Media Pty Ltd
PO Box 1069
Bondi Junction NSW 1355
Australia

contact@flyingelephant.com.au

National Library of Australia Cataloguing-in-Publication data:

Gervay, Susanne.
      Shadows of Olive Trees.
      ISBN 978-0-6482035-4-4.
A823.3

Website: https://sgervay.com

Shadows of Olive Trees - https://www.amazon.com.au/Shadows-Olive-Trees-Susanne-Gervay

Print, ebook, audio

SUSANNE GERVAY

SHADOWS
of Olive Trees

FLYING ELEPHANT MEDIA

It is the 1970s, when young women are discovering their voice, changing, demanding equal rights

Chapter 1

Tessa can't remember when she hasn't retreated behind the brick fence isolating the school in the red-light district. It's an old church inner city school. Expensive. Only girls. Built before the prostitutes, drug dealers, homeless took possession.

Her thick black hair is pulled tightly back. She rubs her hands along her black-ribbed stockings, straightening them, then carefully puts on her regulation hat. She hurries past other girls towards the school. The girls look out of place in their large, blue-rimmed felt bowlers, like escapee bishops. Those hats would have been a penance for the archbishop, but there is no mercy shown to the girls.

Tessa's felt bowler is always worn neatly on her head. She envies her closest friend Athena, who squashes her hat into the smallest of balls and crushes it into her school bag. Only when a teacher appears does Athena unravel the felt ball and place it casually on her head. School rules say the hat has to be worn or there's a detention. Sometimes someone stops Athena, but she never gets a detention, or a new hat. At the end of the day, they walk to the bus stop together. They talk about school and family and the rough sandstone brick terraces they pass with their decaying occupants. There's unconscious irony at a girl their age, standing against 'Power to Women' slashed across the wall of the Church of Christ. Her thin legs are smoothed by clear stockings that disappear into a shiny leather skirt. The girls catch her eye and she calls out laughingly, 'Wanna join me? You can make a lot of money.' Her hand rubs the air.

Tessa looks down as they walk past. She whispers, 'Her stockings aren't like ours.' The girl is occupied now, talking to a man who towers over her. Tessa shudders. 'Is she eighteen, like us?'

Athena shakes her head. 'I don't know.' They walk quickly then, their reflections a precious secret between them.

The bus trip is short, and Tessa watches Athena move away towards her home. They are joined in their Greek ancestry, but Athena is third generation Australian and only speaks Greek to her grandparents. Her parents go on short holidays and leave Athena and her brother to look after the house. Tessa can't imagine her father ever allowing that. Athena has parties and goes to other girls' homes and school camps. Tessa is forbidden. Sometimes she argues with her mother. 'Please, tell me why? Everyone is going. Tell me.' Her mother never answers properly, hiding behind tables and chairs until Tessa shouts. 'It's not fair.' Then her mother cries and Tessa whispers. I'm sorry.' Tessa dares not ask her father. He remembers the village he came from and still looks to the traditions and old ways.

Tessa is allowed her special friend because Athena's parents go to the large white Greek Orthodox church. The church stands firmly planted between the red brick Australian cottages. It would have looked magnificent against the green twisted olive trees on an ancient hillside, but its round basilica and looming towers sit alien among its neighbours.

Sundays are precious to Tessa. She has faith, even when the service is endless. Tessa looks at Athena who sits beside her. Athena nudges her when the priest's hat is crooked or if someone chants out of tune, and they laugh secretly behind their hands.

Sometimes Athena shakes her dark hair and lets her fingers slide slowly through the long strands. Tessa notices men look, until their wives or mothers nudge them back to their prayers. Tessa touches her hair nervously, in anticipation, but no one looks.

This Sunday is special, because Tessa's parents have given her permission to go on a picnic with Athena's family. The service ends and people gather outside for the social talk that is a necessary ritual, inquiring about each other's health and family, talking politics and taxes and church. Athena puts her arm through Tessa's, as they wait for people to complete their observances.

Tessa is relieved to wave goodbye to her parents and her younger brother Peter, who is sixteen. Tessa is relieved that she's not going home to prepare their usual Sunday lunch. She doesn't want to help her mother cook and serve and clear up today. She doesn't want to watch Peter sit with her father at the table expectantly. *I am happy. I'm going on a picnic with Athena.*

Athena's voice is musical as she calls her into the car. They hum to the songs on the radio and Athena rocks against her until they are in rhythm.

The greenness of the park makes a wedge in the suburban sprawl of bricks and mortar. They drive into the park and stop midway between rose gardens and lakes. Athena's parents spread out a blanket on the grass. There is so much food, and they indolently eat roast lamb and buttered rolls. It is the hottest part of the day and Athena's parents lie on their picnic lounge chairs, half dozing.

'We're going for a walk. Is that all right?' Athena asks.

'Go on. Enjoy the park. But don't go too far,' her mother answers.

The sunlight drifts through the trees, making the girls appear dreamlike. Athena's hair glistens in the reflections of the hot rays. They wander past gardens, through trees, following unknown trails far from the blanket and picnic lounge chairs. The girls lean against each other. Tessa puts her arm around Athena's waist. Athena softly murmurs Tessa's name.

Playfully Athena shakes her head, letting the lethargy fall from her. 'Let's go to the lake.' She takes Tessa's hand, pulling her towards the blueness. They run slowly at first, tripping leaves and grass. Then they skip, moving their legs high like show horses cantering, then galloping, then racing, panting, with black manes flicking. They reach the lake's edge breathless; laughing as they fall at the lake's shore.

Athena splashes water on her face, enjoying it trickling down her neck, wetting her blouse. The lake shimmers like sunlight. She lies back at the water's border, heaving unhurriedly, rhythmically.

'Tessa, it's so hot. Come here. Under the willow trees.' Athena's grey eyes entice. Tessa moves towards her friend. They lie in the afternoon sun, whispering of school and parents and Sunday services. They talk about the prostitutes lingering outside the church and, why they linger and what they do in the dark alleys and cheap terrace houses. It makes them hold onto each other, but the sun is hot and their grasp softens into turning, touching, as the fingers of the willows stir around them. They doze, arms entwined, with Tessa's face nestling into Athena's breasts.

***

Monday. Tessa buttons her white school shirt and knots her tie. She pulls too hard. *I hate this.* Tessa loathes the rough material of the blue serge tunic that scratches her skin, making it itchy, raw. She slams her hand against her brother's bedroom door.

'Wake up. It's already eight.'

There's grunting inside. 'Okay. I hear you.'

'It's late. Get up.'

'Say please, Tessa. Please,' Peter laughs.

Tessa slams against his door again. 'I've got things to do you know, Peter.' The household duties never used to disturb her before, but they do now. She hurries to set the table.

Breakfast is an ordered meal, as is every meal. Mr Kassis nods, satisfied with his wife and daughter as he sits at the head of the table and Peter sits on his right. Tessa and Mrs Kassis run to get the food, clear the table, stir the thick black coffee on the stove. It's habitual, automatic, as Tessa moves through her duties, but her thoughts aren't automatic. She thinks of Athena arguing teasingly with her father at the picnic. She glances at her father. *I couldn't argue with you. You'd be so angry.* She shudders as Mrs Kassis brushes past, the black linen of her mother's dress making her skin goose bump. She remembers Athena's mother in a pale rose skirt pushed above her knees, sunbaking in the

5

afternoon heat. *Imagine my mother doing that. Sunbaking.*

Hiding a smile, Tessa gives her father his coffee. Suddenly she turns away as she remembers yesterday, behind the science block. They'd poured over the pages of *The Female Eunuch*. Athena had been so funny reading out all the sex bits, but it had really shocked them.

Tessa brings the fig jam her mother made to the table. She glances at Mrs Kassis, who's finally sitting at the table. *Why don't you drink your coffee? Why don't you ask something for yourself?* Pushing the fig jam in front of her mother, she jerks out a chair and sits beside her. *Well, I'm going to ask.*

'The jam is very good.' Mr Kassis bites into the bread, so that the seeds of the fig catch between his teeth. Mrs Kassis smiles.

Be calm. You're not asking for much. She starts. 'Papa. I really liked the picnic with Athena.'

'You had a good time?' He determinedly finishes his coffee. There are problems with a machine at his furniture factory. He works long hours and sometimes at night he nods to sleep in his armchair with the newspaper falling beside him. Then Mrs Kassis wakes him gently and they walk together up the staircase to their bedroom. Tessa helps with the accounts at the end of each week and on Saturdays Peter works on the factory floor screwing wood into wood. Mr Kassis refuses to use the glue that's cheaper and easier. He'd be ashamed of making bad furniture.

'Can I ask you something, Papa?' Her dark eyes flit from her father's face to her plate. She feels her

6

stomach knot. He nods impatiently. *Don't be stupid, Tessa. You're not asking for the world. Everyone is allowed to have friends over. I want to too.* 'Can I invite Athena over? To return her parents 'hospitality,' she adds hurriedly.

Tessa is rarely allowed friends to visit, but Mr Kassis understands hospitality. He stops to deliberate. Slowly he stands, then looks at his daughter. 'Yes, it is right. Athena may come, but only after your exams.'

'After the exams? Why do I have to wait so long?'

'Tessa, I cannot talk about this. The big machine is broken.' He turns to Peter. 'After your school, I need you to help me in the factory today.'

Peter grunts because his mouth is full of fig jam. Mr Kassis' face creases into worry lines and Tessa can't pressure him now. He pushes his chair away, leaving his wife and daughter to clear the breakfast plates.

'Athena 's coming over, Mama.' *I don't care that he's said later. He said yes. Yes.* Tessa hums *All You Need Is Love* as she wipes the dark oak table that's always stood in the middle of their kitchen. Mrs Kassis hums with her until they're wiping and humming around the table.

Peter shouts over them. 'You can't sing.'

Mrs Kassis stops but Tessa sings louder. *All you Need Is Love ... Love ... Love...*' until Peter blocks his ears with his hands.

'Come on, we'll really be late.' Tessa throws the tea towel on the sink, kisses her mother in a flurry and grabs her bag, singing *All You Need is Love* all the way out of the house until Peter's ready to murder her. Then she's quiet. *I'm happy. Athena is coming over. Athena.* Peter's irritating comments don't irritate her today and she runs her fingers around the inside of her collar to stop the chafing of her uniform. There's a new splash of graffiti on the Church of Christ: 'Women have rights too.' Peter thinks the graffiti is funny. 'You're so ignorant, Peter.' But she's not interested in arguing today and leaves him laughing.

***

Where's Athena? She's anxious as she crosses the bitumen courtyard, where the girls usually meet. Tessa stands still, turning to look left, then right, then left, then sees Athena. Friends are chatting to her as the bell rings. Everyone wanders towards the classrooms. Tessa can't concentrate in Science. Miss Newland stands in the front of the classroom, a thin, pale lady but flushed now. No one pays attention. One girl starts making animal noises. Other girls copy until the class sounds like a farmyard. The red of Miss Newland's face gets redder. There's snickering.

Miss Newland flees the classroom saying she won't teach such animals and there's laughing. Some girls look down at their desks, embarrassed. Tessa coughs acid into her mouth and runs to the toilet block. She rinses her mouth with water, spitting it into the stain- less steel basin. Then she hears crying. It's Miss Newland, locked in a toilet cubicle. Tessa quietly leaves.

The bell goes for lunch and Tessa presses Athena's arm as she moves out of the classroom. 'Can you come to my house on a Saturday, after the exams are over?' Athena half hears as girls crowd around her. 'Come on,' she says to Tessa. 'We're eating next to the tennis court.'

They all sit with their sandwiches and salads. Tessa takes out the feta cheese and thick bread her mother packed for her. She hopes they don't notice her lunch, as they talk about teachers and exams and who they are going out with and how far they've gone. 'But I'd never go the whole way,' one of the girls says. I'm going to wait until I'm married.'

Sex. Tessa shudders.

'Then you'll have to wait a long time, because we've got a lot to do before we get married.' Athena flicks back her dark hair. 'Don't you want to travel? I want to try a few different foods at least' She bites into a red apple. 'Maybe I'll eat a sheep's head in Iceland.' They laugh. Athena winks at Tessa. 'There's too much to do first.'

Yes. You're right. Tessa admires Athena sitting there among those girls who think they are so free, so different. *Married. How can they even think about it?* Her cousin flickers into her thoughts. Twenty and engaged. Arranged by the parents. *I'll never do that.* She looks curiously at the girls eating their lunches. *My cousin's doing what's expected, but you're free to do what you like. Why would you waste that?*

No one asks Tessa her thoughts, because she's not part of their days at school. She doesn't share their lives outside the red brick fence. But if they'd known her, she might have told them about a girl standing against the walls of the Church of Christ, or about the power between a man and a woman, or amazing new ideas from women. Germaine Greer and Simone de Beauvoir. Smiling, she remembers a hot afternoon lying beneath wispy willows and a shimmering lake. *I'd never tell you about that.*

Tessa watches Athena. The bell goes again. As they walk to class, Tessa whispers, 'So will you come to visit, after the exams?'

'Of course, I'll come.' Then Athena joins the other girls, but Tessa doesn't feel left behind. She'll have Athena to herself for more than the bus journey home, more than the half-disturbed whisperings in the church. Athena will be hers for a whole day.

***

The girls are cruel to Miss Newland, but Tessa isn't. She remembers the teacher locked in the toilet cubicle. Miss Newland is leaving at the end of the term. Tessa writes a card to her.

All the classes are quiet, orderly now. No one dares disturb the inevitable push towards the final exams. The only break from the pressure is Speech Day, the last school day before the exams. Tessa's and Athena's parents sit together, well dressed, expectant. The final-year girls line the hall to listen to speeches. Athena wins the English prize and Tessa's parents applaud. Tessa wins no prizes.

Athena is head girl, so she speaks to the audience like all head girls have done for as long as the school has existed. Even in her uniform she has a magnetism that makes the audience stop their whisperings. Her grey eyes capture them in dreams of the future. Her tie and shirt and school trappings don't restrict her, as she spreads her hands outwards. 'There are new and exciting challenges for women today. Women are entering law, medicine, engineering, business and, most importantly, they're exploring life.'

Many of the girls cry in the school hall. Athena cries and the headmistress puts her arms around her. Tessa cries too, in anticipation, because she will leave the red brick fence and blue serge uniforms and walk past the prostitutes and drug dealers and be part of a world which is at least different. 'Grant me at least a new servitude,' Tessa says under her breath. She remembers Athena arguing with her over Jane Eyre's words in the library.

'Tessa, women don't have to serve.'

'But I do.'

Athena had scoffed. 'My parents come from Greek background too. So I know. You don't have to.'

'That's unfair. You know how traditional my family is. It's like the Greek village is here. I'm Jane Eyre at home.'

Athena had been angry. 'Did you miss International Women's Year last year?'

'Don't, Athena.' Tessa had turned away, hurt.

'The final exams are exhausting: studying at night, sleeping restlessly, waking to her family's expectations and then the long day. The plastic chairs sweat in the school hall in the November heat. Or is it Tessa's sweat? Athena sits two seats across with her head bent down, writing furiously. The hall is big, isolating as the teachers march between the wooden desks checking for cheats and liars. Tessa doesn't need to cheat because she's studied until the information solidified into heavy immovable facts inside her head. The exams end. *Thank God*. Tessa shoves the plastic chair under the desk. There's excitement. Girls are going away for holidays.

There are parties and celebrations. Tessa pretends she doesn't care, that there won't be any parties for her. Exam results will be afterwards. She's sure that Athena will get into Philosophy, 'So I'll be a thinking, journalist,' Athena had laughed. Tessa will get into Arts and the librarian diploma that follows it.

It's the last day of school. Girls hug, kiss, write their names in chalk on classroom blackboards. Tessa walks out of the wooden gates, past the school brick fence. She swings her school bag, humming to herself, kicking a newspaper flapping along the street. She looks at the discarded needle lying under it, and edges it with her laced black school shoes into the curb. The day is warm and she notices a man leaning over the wrought iron lace balcony, in a white singlet and navy shorts. Tessa imagines a blacksmith with his huge hammer forcing hot iron into the intricate patterns of the balustrade. Machines do it now, like in her father's factory.

She stops, slowly surveying the street with its inner-city confusion. The rough, handmade convict bricks of the terraces and the abrasive corner store with its aluminium windows and neon signs; the old, old lady who's lived there all her life and the young, young girl selling sex for heroin; the Church of Christ and the brothels. This is a street Tessa has known most of her life, coming to and from school. Suddenly there's fear as she realizes she's leaving it. Tessa throws her bag onto the bitumen. 'No. No, I am not scared. I'm not scared.' She grabs her blue felt, hat, squashes it into the smallest of balls and, with the pleasure of a juggler, flings it into a council garbage bin along the roadside.

Chapter 2

The special Saturday comes. Tessa has made a chocolate cake. She cleans and recleans her room, then sits waiting at her window upstairs. She sees Athena and runs to open the door. Athena laughs. 'I haven't even rung the doorbell.' Taking her hand, Tessa pulls her inside.

Mr Kassis waits rigidly in his armchair. No one else dares sit in it. Athena enters the lounge room. She's wearing a white cotton blouse and a soft yellow skirt that flows loosely around her legs. She seems to startle Mr Kassis. It's like a warm breeze entering the old-fashioned room with its heavy carpets and ornately wrought ornaments. The room stifles Tessa. She hates the family occasions, when she has to sit on the floral settee.

'Hello, Mr Kassis. Hello, Mrs Kassis. It's nice to see you. My mother sends her best wishes.' Mrs Kassis smiles. Mr Kassis nods. 'You're kind to invite me to visit. My father told me to thank you.' Athena hands Mr Kassis a box of homemade biscuits. 'My mother baked them for you. They're delicious.'

Mr Kassis accepts the biscuits, waiting for Athena to settle. Athena chats as Mr Kassis passes the box of biscuits to Mrs Kassis for their morning tea. He remembers the girl receiving a prize at Speech Day, applauding her success. Now he observes her carefully, listening to her talk about her family and her future. He nods at her words, listening a little more intently, bending forward out of his chair, pressing his hand against the arm rest. Her words weave curiously into his thoughts, like strange threads. Her long dark hair falls back as she laughs. He enjoys the movement of the pale gold of her skirt and wonders why he listens to only a girl. He watches the gold cloth cling and float like her words.

Athena suddenly stops, jolting Mr Kassis back into his chair. 'I'm disturbing you, Mr Kassis. I'd better go up with Tessa to her room.'

'We will have coffee first.' Mr Kassis gets up from his chair and motions to Athena to sit in it. He turns to his wife. 'Mrs Kassis we will have coffee. Tessa, help your mother.' Tessa closes her lips tightly so that he doesn't hear her *no*. She stamps out of the room. *Papa can't keep Athena there forever.* Tessa and her mother prepare the morning meal in the kitchen. Tessa slams cups into saucers until her mother tells her to stop. 'You will disturb everyone, Tessa.'

'It's not fair.' Her mother pretends she doesn't understand. They hear Mr Kassis laugh while Athena's voice teases and plays. When Tessa and her mother re-enter the lounge room with the coffee and biscuits laid carefully on the silver service, Mr Kassis is sitting on the floral settee. The coffee is poured and the biscuits served to Mr Kassis' approval. They eat and drink until Mr Kassis allows them to go upstairs. 'Enjoy the afternoon, girls.' He smiles, making Tessa ashamed of her ungratefulness.

Tessa's never had a real friend visit her room before, only distant cousins and relatives and sometimes Peter. Athena laughs. 'Stop moving around Tessa. You 're like a mouse.'

'It's just that I want to show you everything.' She takes her golden icon of Jesus from her desk and gives it to Athena. 'My parents gave it to me when I was born.'

'I had one too, but I don 't know where mine is.' She's half-apologetic.

'Can I show you something else?' Tessa moves towards her shelf. They're called Starry Moons. I love the name. They're like a smooth amber snail, but hard and shiny. Can you see the pink inside?' Athena picks one up. 'I collected them from a sandy beach one summer, a long time ago. The beach was really hot. No one else would walk on the sand, except me.' She cradles a Starry Moon in her hand. 'The sand was cool near the sea. We were visiting some cousins. I loved the water and look what it gave me.'

'You have so many shells, Tessa.'

'I've been collecting them forever. This one is a frog shell.'

'It's awful with all those bumps and lumps. Look at the orange inside. Oh no, are there teeth there?' Athena drops the shell into Tessa's hands.

'It won't eat you.' They laugh a little. Tessa confides. 'I really want to share all my shells with you, Athena.

I've never shown anyone else before.' Tessa puts shell after shell into Athena's palms, touching together the curves and cones and shiny silver bits, experiencing the roughness and smoothness.

The shells ease them into intimacy and they lie on the bed holding them, talking about their futures. 'I wonder what university will be like, Athena? '

Athena rolls onto her back, holding up a spiral Glory of the Sea. 'Exciting. You'll do really well in literature.'

'I don't think so. The best grade I ever got was B.' Athena's grey eyes catch the light. 'Yes, but that's at school. It'll be different at university. Not so many rules and you'll get to read a lot more of the books you want to.' Athena turns around, still holding the Glory of the Sea.

'Papa says I have to be a librarian in a school.'

Tessa mimics him. "It is such a good profession, for when you have children." It'll make me worth a lot more as well, when he sells me off to the highest bidder. Come on men, buy this good little Greek girl. Great teeth, nice mane of hair, good at cooking and cleaning and, thrown in for nothing, a university degree.'

'Don't be stupid.' Athena gives Tessa the shell.

'Sorry, that sounds awful.' Tessa bends her head, so that Athena can't see her face. 'It's just that my parents are so happy about my cousin getting married. And she'll be pregnant soon, and they keep talking about her. How she makes her parents proud and all that.' Closing her eyes, Tessa whispers, 'I run out of the room when they go on about her.'

'It's your cousin's choice, and you're not your cousin.'

'No, I'll be a librarian and it'll be like I'm back at school again.' Tessa bites her nail. 'I don't want that either.' She waits. 'Do you remember Miss Newland?'

'Why?'

'Miss Newland cried in the toilets after the girls were cruel to her one day. Imagine being a grown-up woman and locking yourself in a toilet cubicle.' She looks at Athena. I'm scared that'll be me one day.'

'Tessa, it won't be. You're not Miss Newland. You're not your cousin. You don't have to be her or anyone else.'

Tessa pushes her thick black hair away from her face. 'I loved studying *A Doll's House*.' She pauses. 'It's hard to believe Ibsen wrote it a hundred years ago. Imagine, Nora was allowed to be more than a wife and mother. She had the right to think for herself.'

'You know, you can be a Nora too.'

Tessa shakes her head. 'Papa wouldn't understand. I have to do what he says. He's worked so hard to give me and my brother everything. And I know my life's really easy. I feel selfish.' Tessa pauses. 'I love books and being in a library is better than being my cousin.'

'Is it Tessa?' Athena watches her. 'You know, you're not asking permission to be an axe murderer by wanting something different.'

Tessa takes a deep breath. 'I'd feel like one, if I didn't do what Papa wanted.'

'Come on, Tessa.' Athena shakes her head. Tell me what you'd really like to do.'

'I can't.' Athena shuffles closer to her on the bed. Tessa feels her friend's warmth. 'If I say, you've got to promise not to tell anyone else.' Athena nods. 'All right then. I want to think, do philosophy or even archaeology. Maybe become a writer, like you.'

Athena sits up. 'That'll be great. We can write about the world and everything together.' She grabs Tessa's arm. 'Don't be a coward. Just tell your father.'

'That's me, a great coward. I'm not brave like you. Sometimes I think you're like St Joan, except you don't get burned at the stake.'

Athena laughs, her musical laugh. 'St Joan. I hope not. Fire is for cooking and romantic nights or for midnight feasts. Come on, let's imagine what we'll be doing when we're famous reporters.' Tessa's dark eyes gleam. 'Let's imagine. What about going to Africa and saving rhinos? Or what about being the first women writers to report on a lost tribe in the Amazon?'

'Can we visit the Greek Islands, Athena?'

'Yes, we can do anything, Tessa. Anything.'

They start, slowly at first, naming other places around the world, then places no one's heard of, made-up names, made-up places, speaking quicker and quicker, letting ideas crash and rise until their minds are racing and their words unable to keep up. Until they feel like energy; until they are silent, lying beside each other with their thoughts.

Tessa turns towards her. 'My parents deserve respect. I want to do what they want. Obey them.' She catches her breath. 'It's just,' she hesitates, 'I'm suffocating. The priest tells me to be a good daughter. To obey too.' She whispers. 'I'm sick of obeying.' Tessa fists her hands. 'I love my parents and I know I'm lucky. So why does it all hurt?' She hits the bed. 'What's wrong with me? Can't I just accept? Be happy?'

Athena puts her hands over Tessa's. 'You can be happy.'

'I don't know how.' Her eyes question. 'I feel ugly.' Athena stares at Tessa. She shakes her head. 'You're beautiful.'

'I'm plain, Athena.'

Athena pulls her to the dresser. 'Look at yourself.' She combs Tessa's thick hair so that it curls teasingly around her face. She smooths lipstick on Tessa's soft lips, then fingers redness onto her cheeks. 'You're special, Tessa.'

Tessa stares into the mirror as if watching Athena with a stranger, watching Athena stroke a stranger's hair, a stranger's cheek. *Is that me? Me?*

Athena outlines Tessa's lips with her fingers, then with her lips. There is a sweetness in the taste as Athena presses her lips against Tessa's.

They lie again on the bed. Athena moves her hands across Tessa's breasts. It doesn't feel wrong. Slowly Tessa strokes Athena's body. Athena loosens her white cotton blouse and presses Tessa's hands against her nipples. It doesn't feel wrong. Virgins of the church and their parents, they touch, explore, search. There is deep pleasure in release. It feels like love.

Chapter 3

The vacation is long, humid, filled with a mindlessness that makes Tessa want to walk the decayed streets that surround her old school. She does not walk those streets. Instead she helps her mother in the kitchen, around the house, at the shops buying fruit and milk. 'Mama, I'll carry that.' 'Yes, Mama the pears are fresh today.' 'I'll put the flowers in the vase, Mama.' In the afternoons they drink tea together.

Sundays are restless too. The priest chants words Tessa believes, but she misses Athena, who has gone overseas for a holiday. She closes her eyes, imagining Athena's there, only to open them and find Peter sitting next to her in the church.

The garden is Tessa's pleasure. Sometimes she digs with fury, wildly planting, potting, pruning, turning the earth. At other times she rests, smelling the jasmine and lavender and rose petals, watching her mother flustered by the sun and the myriad of flowers. Tessa kisses her then and takes the flowers from her hands.

Tessa's planted a fragrant magnolia. The creamy white flowers emerging from felted pods make her think of Athena. Mr and Mrs Kassis like their daughter gardening because it reminds them of their villages and the land that was pivotal to that life. Mr Kassis praises her. 'You are a good girl.'

Tessa loves to please her father. She remembers him putting her on his shoulders as a little girl so that she could see the Anzac Day Parade. The whole family would watch the soldiers marching, their medals shining in the Australian sun. He was so proud of the Greek contingent. Mr Kassis' father had fought for the Allies in World War II.

There are other memories too - hiding behind her father 's broad back when she was afraid to go to school. He'd said 'I promise you will be safe. You will learn at school Tessa' and he'd given her two sweets. 'For later.' Sometimes she sits at his feet and he talks about fishing in the seas around his island in a wooden boat, and the olive trees that surrounded his village. He tells about people long dead and they feel like part of Tessa'-s life. She wishes she had known them.

Her father misses his homeland.

Tessa resents the weekends. The ritual visits to and from relatives, the old, old women sitting in their black widowed garb, eating delicacies Mrs Kassis and Tessa labour over. Some have no teeth and Tessa wants to scream at them. *You live in Australia. You can get new teeth.* But she just serves the food and strong black coffee.

The women sit and talk about children and knitting and how to keep the house clean and Tessa thinks she'll go mad. She runs to her room, locking the door. She throws herself onto her schoolgirl bed and cries. *Athena, where are you?* but there's no Athena. Just home and routine. Even Christmas does not relieve the monotony. Two months to wait before university begins.

Athena doesn't answer. Tessa lies staring at the ceiling, trying to pray to her icon for patience, holding her smooth shells, trying to remember that the afternoon will end. Slowly, she stands up from her bed and goes to the window. The leaves of the trees rustle

21

in the park opposite. She thinks of them as her trees. Tessa straightens her dress, turns to her door and walks back downstairs.

'Where have you been?' Peter digs at her. 'Mum's been looking for you.'

'Why don't you help her sometimes?' 'Sure, Tessa.'

Tessa hates the sarcasm in his voice. 'Shut up Peter. I do help her.' She turns away from him.

***

Mr Kassis insists on taking his daughter to enrol at the university. His factory can do without him for one day. The enrolment line crawls through the corridor, down steps, trailing onto grassy lawns. Mr Kassis is not impatient. Uncoiling his hands, he puts them into his pockets. He stands erect, moving his head, slowly surveying, savouring this place of education.

As a child, his parents had had enough to feed the family. He had not minded running barefoot down the rocky cliffs to the sea. His feet had hardened as he grew. He remembers his hidden hopes - to learn, to study books. He had left school as a boy - eleven years old. Even then he was really a man. Looking at Tessa standing beside him, he nods. 'I am glad I give you this opportunity to learn.' Tessa stares at her feet.

Mr Kassis takes his hands from his pockets and looks at them - tough, leathery fisherman's hands. His father and he, had hauled heavy fish into the boat and sewn torn fishing nets. The horizon stopped where the father's boat anchored. His parents never left their island, their shimmering sea. But the boy saw beyond. He didn't want to grow old and wither, eking out life under the harsh Grecian sun. 'Australia is a good country,' Mr Kassis says aloud.

Tessa rubs her hands along her skirt, like at school. She focuses on the end of the line where a bureaucrat fills in paper. The bureaucratic woman is all Tessa can see, all she wants to see. Pretend he's not here. *He's not standing here. I'm alone.* She's ashamed of her father standing beside her. Her turn comes to enrol. She fills in forms while her father nods approval.

Afterwards they walk past the stalls that entice students to join the drama society and the math club and the cavers. Mr Kassis looks into the lecture halls where Tessa will sit, and touches the books Tessa will read. He forces her to follow him, forces her to listen to him, forces her to see the learning he wanted so much. The learning he could never have. Slowly Tessa's anger dissipates. She slides her arm through his.

When they arrive home there's celebration. Mrs Kassis has prepared Tessa's favourite foods. A feast of biscuits and baklava. She knows her mother has worked all day to prepare this for her. 'You're too good to me.' She hugs her mother and Mrs Kassis is content.

***

Tessa starts classes only in the second week. Mr Kassis says she doesn't need to join the clubs or meet the other students. The activities of orientation week are irrelevant to Mr Kassis, so his daughter won't go. 'You will help your mother.' Tessa forces her lips to lift. It looks like a smile. It looks like acceptance.

She quietly goes to her room. Locks the door. She lifts her arms high above her head, stretching so that she's tall. She wants to be big, powerful, an adult. With a quick jerk she tugs her brown jumper over her head and throws it onto the floor. She unzips her skirt too quickly. It catches her skin, leaving a red line on the side of her waist. The clasp of her bra catches too, then releases.

Her breasts are heavy as she cups them, kneading until the, nipples stand erect. Then she pushes her white cotton pants to the floor, exposing black hair trailing upwards in a fine line to her navel.

Tessa stares at herself in the mirror. Her body looks vulnerable, soft. She pounds her thighs, patterning red hand marks along her legs and hips. 'My body,' she whispers. 'Mine.'

It's warm outside but she slides under her blankets because she's cold, stinging. The coldness makes her shake. University has started and she's afraid. There are red brick fences, but they aren't school fences. Where do they come from? Tessa cries into her pillow because she knows the father she loves is building them.

Chapter 4

Mr Kassis has already left for work. Mrs Kassis stands at the front door waiting for Tessa to leave for her first day at university. She presses her forehead with the back of her hand. She was twelve when she left her small village school to tend the vegetables and help her mother prepare conserves and spin the soft wool of the goats. Their home was small, not like her house now.

'I never imagined that my daughter would go to the university. It makes me very happy, Tessa. I want it so much for you.'

Tessa hugs her mother. 'I love you.'

She gets off the bus several stops before the university entrance. As she walks through the narrow streets that encircle the university grounds she feels an old familiarity. There are no prostitutes, no drug dealers, but there are young people dressed in the uniform of non-conformity. Short skirts and long skirts and black, holed stockings; boyish earrings and girlish cropped hair; lacey tops and tight blue jeans. She looks down at her grey pleated skirt and black shoes. *I look ridiculous*. Then she laughs. At least it isn't a blue serge tunic.

She lingers, enjoying the nostalgia of terraced houses compressing against each other. As she passes, she glances up at their balconies. There are no middle-aged men in singlets drinking beer, only youthful occupants restoring iron lattice work while they undergo modern revelation and self-discovery. She laughs aloud. *I want revelation*. She starts to run.

Tessa's puffing as she enters the sandstone gates and slows to catch her breath. The historic buildings of the quadrangle loom ahead. When the bells from the tower start pealing she giggles. It's like a prophetic sign from one of her Gothic novels. Tessa ignores the multistorey library with its pragmatism. She knows the modern library is important and she'll spend hours there studying, but for now she wants to enjoy the romance of strolling through the quadrangle, between arches and up wooden staircases to her first literature class. She's excited. It's going to be held in the oldest lecture room in the university.

Seats slope up in rows and Tessa slots herself near a centre aisle. The old wooden benches have been initialled and reinstalled by rebels of other times. There are angry scribblings of rejected lovers and bored students and besotted love notes from long lost lovers signed with forgotten initials. She smiles. Tessa fingers the deep cuts. 'Shakespeare sucks', 'Tennis Tennyson?', 'Dope, Coleridge?'. More graffiti. Tessa thinks she should be disgusted, but isn't. The graffiti isn't as interesting as what's splashed across the walls of the Church of Christ.

Professor Davids bolts into the hall. His hair is dishevelled, his black moustache careless. Tessa bites her lip, because he looks like an older Heathcliff from *Wuthering Heights*. Tessa blushes, trying to stop memories of midnight fantasies of Heathcliff flitting between fresh sheets and her white lecture pad. The professor hits the lectern. 'Truth. Sex. Eternity. Laughter. Sorrow.' His blue eyes pierce the silent audience. He points to a student. 'Where can I find all this?' The student moves uncomfortably on the bench while those next to him look down, hoping the professor won't notice them. 'Well?'

'Feelings,' the unlucky student eventually stammers.

'Thank you, Sir.' Professor Davids surveys the lecture hall. 'Feelings or intellect or the passions of humanity. Poetry is the inner crystallisation of human emotions and thought. That's what we will be exploring.'

Tessa scribbles in her pad. 'Professor Davids'.

'Idiot,' Tessa hears someone in front say. Professor Davids enjoys the performance, making the podium a theatre where he's actor, director, creator. She's mesmerised by his movements, which exaggerate his height and lengthen his arms as they expand and contract with his arguments. He recites John Donne.

Death, be not proud, though some have called thee
Mighty and dreadful, for thou art not so;
For those whom thou think'st thou dost overthrow
Die not, poor Death, nor yet canst thou kill me.
...
One short sleep past, we wake eternally
And death shall be no more; Death, thou shalt die.

'Death' reverberates in her mind. John Donne 's certainty in God and eternal life overpowering death makes her think of her icon, and of evening services chanting immortality and salvation.

Suddenly Professor Davids becomes soft, vulnerable as he reveals Elizabeth Barrett Browning's love for her husband.

How do I love thee?

Let me count the ways.
I love thee to the depth and breadth and height
My soul can reach, when feeling out of sight
For the ends of Being and ideal Grace.

...

I love thee with the breath,
Smiles, tears, of all my life; and, if God Choose,
I shall but love thee better after death.

Tessa bends her head because she's seen her parents' marriage.

Professor Davids questions. 'Death. Love. They seem such different pans of human experience. Are they?'

Tessa watches Professor Davids control the stage and the students, playing with them, making them think. She remembers the stumbling readings and prescribed interpretations of school. Pressing her hands against the wooden bench, she whispers. 'I'm glad I'm here.' The lecture ends with a challenge from Samuel Johnson that lingers between the students, as they scramble out of the hall. *The mind... neglects truths that lie open before her.*

***

Tessa moves with the crowd towards the quadrangle noticeboard to sign up for tutorials. She hears students comment about Professor Davids. Some hate him. Others love him. Others just want to pass the subject. Tessa edges past them. It's a first-in, first-served system. She scribbles her name on Professor Davids' tutorial list.

Tessa jumps when there's a tug on Tessa's sleeve. 'Hi, Tessa. Are you doing poetry as well?'

It's a school friend, no, an acquaintance; a girl from another class who had always seemed sunburnt and bleached. 'Yes, with Professor Davids.' Tessa feels strange because at school Jenny Donovan hadn't spoken to her, except maybe a quick hello, goodbye.

'It's great to see someone I know. Do you want to have lunch?'

'Me?'

Jenny jokes. 'Well I'm not asking Professor Davids, am I?'

Tessa thought she'd sit alone at lunchtime, eating the thickly cut sandwiches with chunks of feta her mother made. 'Yes, that'd be good.' Tessa smiles. She'll have someone to talk to.

***

Tessa sings to herself on her way home. This is better. 'Better, better, better,' she sings aloud as she swings her bag.

***

Her father doesn't question her about her timetable, because university hours are different to school. Teachers and parents can't check and recheck Tessa's movements and thoughts. There's more time, more room to move.

Tessa meets Jenny most days for coffee in the cafeteria. The talk is usually excited, especially when it's about Jenny's current boyfriend or her voluntary work at the women's refuge near the university. Tessa went with her there once. It scared her. The women and children hiding from violent men, in terraces that were peeling and had only cold water. She was glad to go home to her mother's cooking and her father's protection.

Jenny draws Tessa into her friendship group, where they study in the library and debate assignments in the 'talking room'. Afterwards, students meet on the front lawns in front of the quadrangle to discuss lectures and relationships and university life. Jenny and Tessa lie in their special place on the lawn.

'We're having a painting day at the refuge on Saturday. Anyway, the local hardware store's donated brushes, rollers and plenty of paint. So, are you going to help this time?'

Tessa shifts uncomfortably onto her side. She's never told Jenny about the restrictions of her home. It'd be hard to get away on the weekend. She bites her nails because she's ashamed of something else. The refuge frightens her. I'm busy Saturday. Sorry.'

'You've always got an excuse.'

'Saturday's a family day.' She blushes. 'I suppose you think that's a pathetic excuse.'

'It is really. Where do women and children go without a place like that?'

'Look, I agree with you. I just can't be there Saturday.'

Jenny jumps up and brushes the grass from her jeans. Her voice is angry. 'I've got lectures.' She turns away from Tessa.

I'm such a coward. Tessa grabs Jenny 's sleeve as she starts to walk away. *I don't want to be that.* Shaking her head, she forces her words. 'Wait, Jenny. Wait. Please.'

Jenny stops. 'Well?'

Letting go of Jenny 's sleeve, she stammers. 'You're going to the refuge on Wednesday afternoon, aren't you? I've got nothing on then.' Hesitatingly, Tessa asks, 'Can I come with you? I'll paint.'

A huge smile lights. up Jenny's face. 'Yes, Tessa. Yes.'

***

The weekends at home are harder. Tessa wants to help her mother in the kitchen, but resents it more than ever. She fights with Peter more, who complains to her father. 'I want to talk to you in the sitting room,' Mr Kassis demands.

She sits on the floral settee awkwardly. 'You have changed since university began. Why is this?'

'Papa, I haven't changed. It's just that there's lots of study.'

'Yes, but you shout at your brother. You hurt your mother.'

Tessa bites her nail. She doesn't care that Peter is annoyed, but she cares that she hurts her mother who makes her sandwiches and loves her. 'I try to help my mother.' She stops biting her nail. 'It's just that Peter isn't fair. He leaves his stuff around and I'm supposed to pick it up. He expects everyone else to do things for him.'

'I do not want to listen to this. You do your duties and be grateful. You are a girl and you are going to university because I allow it. I could never go.'

She looks down.

'I can see you are sorry. You are a good girl.'

I'm not sorry. Don't you see, Papa. I'm not a good girl. When will the weekend finish?

She runs to her room and lies on her bed. She always used to plod through her school work. It was as if the blue felt bowler were the circumference of her

31

thoughts. Neat, controlled, ordered thoughts. But university requires no hat. There are no judges, *I can choose. Choose.* Choices, and commitment to those choices. She's interested in geography and education, but it's literature that challenges the limits she knew at school.

***

The tutorials with Professor Davids are intimidating. Twelve of them sit around a horseshoe of desks. Tessa always sits beside the same girl, next to the window. She feels the breeze that runs through the quadrangle, tinkling between the university bells. Tessa is careful to prepare her work. Once when a student arrived without his reading done, Professor Davids had been sarcastic. 'Obviously you're a literary psychic. You can sense what's in a book without opening the covers. Is that right? Can you sense what's in my mind?' The student hadn't answered. 'No? Not so psychic then.' He'd looked at all of them. 'Tutorials only function, when everyone shares ideas with each other. This young man is using your work when he arrives, without doing his reading.' The professor had motioned to the door and the student had crept out. The tutorials are like his lectures except more intense. He reads Shelley, Keats. Today, he culminates in Coleridge's *Kubla Khan*.

> *But oh! that deep romantic chasm which slanted*
> *Down the green hill athwart a cedarn cover!*
> *A savage place! as holy and enchanted*
> *As e'er beneath a waning moon was haunted*
> *By woman wailing for her demon lover!*

Tessa glances at Professor Davids, whose dark hair carelessly falls across his forehead. So different to her father who always wets his hair, plastering it into order. Tessa looks quickly down at her writing pad, because she doesn't want to be noticed. But the professor does notice her. 'What does that mean to you?' He's never chosen her before. She's embarrassed, as all the students in the tutorial stare at her. Tessa doesn't answer.

'You don't want to answer? Or you can't?' He waits impatiently. Two students flap their hands in the air. 'Right, you've been in my tutorials long enough to know silence is unacceptable. You don't belong here. Another tutorial group will suit you.' He turns to a student with a flapping hand.

The girl beside her writes on Tessa's pad. 'It'll be alright.' Tessa looks at her. But it's not all right. She grits her teeth. Athena would answer. Athena would have courage. Even Jenny wouldn't take it. *You're not my father. You're not Heathcliff. You don't even know me and you judge me like that. It's not fair. Not fair. No.* She calls out. 'Professor Davids, I don't want to go to another tutorial.'

He swings around. 'All right. Well?'

She speaks quietly at first. 'I think it's... passionate, sexual, maybe; frightening '. She looks questioningly at him. 'There's ... Maybe its rawness and... ' she pauses, trying to think of the words that still hang in the room. 'chasm', 'savage', 'wailing',

'It's the demon lover.'

'Is it only woman?'

33

'No, it's more. It's man and woman. Power over each other.'

Professor Davids nods and moves on to other students. The girl next to her smiles but Tessa feels exposed, not like in her mirror in her bedroom, but naked in front of everyone. Can they see her heavy breasts, her thighs, the curling black hairs?

The tutorial ends. Professor Davids comments to students as they leave. He strides over to Tessa. 'Tessa, is it?' She nods. 'Poetry is looking deeply into yourself, the people around you, the universe. It's exhilarating if you want to go on the real journey. Do you want to go on it? '

'Yes,' she stammers, 'but I feel ignorant.'

'We all are. You're starting in the right place.'

Afterwards, Tessa sits on the university lawn listening to someone practising on the grand organ in the ceremonial hall. Students graduate in that hall, and professors have morning teas with important people, and the chamber quartet will be playing there at lunchtime tomorrow.

Jenny Donovan's finished her tutorial too. She slumps down beside Tessa. 'Disgusting, didn't understand a word, but I like my tutor. He's cute.'

Tessa smiles. 'That's a pretty non-academic approach.'

'It's called sex appeal.'

'Well, I wouldn't call Professor Davids cute. He scares me to death, but he's a great teacher. He makes me think about.' Tessa puts her hand over her heart melodramatically, 'The meaning of life.'

'Boring. I'm not interested in dead poets and their meaning.'

'It's not boring,' Tessa grins. 'I was nearly thrown out of my tutorial. Stop laughing. It wasn't funny at the time. If I want to stay in his tutorial. Stop laughing, Jenny. I have to contribute a lot. Are you going to listen?' Jenny's laughing so much that she doesn't hear. Tessa starts too. They both laugh and laugh, lying on the grass.

Poetry and literature don't interest Jenny, but she struggles through it with Tessa's help. Jenny's discovered that Tessa's conservative clothes aren't Tessa. They stroll towards the library to look up references for an assignment. Tessa enjoys touching the books. The independence to choose what she studies. It's harder here, but better than school, better than home. Tessa leaves the university smiling, but as she gets closer to home her stomach knots.

She opens the front door to Mrs Kassis, who wipes her floured hands on her apron and kisses her. daughter. 'How was the university? ' She waits expectantly for news.

Tessa feels an obligation to her mother. She tells her about Jenny and her tutorial, but nothing about the intimacy she feels at finding Jenny, or the sensuality of Coleridge's poetry, or the freedom of lying on the university lawn.

'A letter has come for you. It is from Athena.' Tessa hugs her mother, then runs upstairs with it refusing to look at her mother. She closes her eyes. *I want this all to myself. I'm sorry, Mama. Sorry.* She lies on her bed and reads.

Dearest Tessa

Even though it's winter now in Greece, the weather has been freakish. It's warm and everything sparkles, glistens. I love it. I wish you were here of course. I drove with my cousin from Athens through the countryside right to the shores of the Mediterranean Sea. The land is rugged, like a man. It's a male country. That's a sexist thing to say, but I feel the masculinity everywhere.

We found this rocky outcrop -. half island, half mainland - jutting into sea, jutting into sky. They call it Monemvassia.

We walked across a causeway, upwards over rocks to a walled city. We had to enter through a narrow doorway. It was like going back in time. There were narrow cobblestone streets with women in black, leading donkeys. Men sat drinking strong coffee and ouzo in small coffee houses. We kept climbing upwards, past stone houses roughly joined together, past ancient women spinning greyish- white wool, past men kneading worry beads. I thought we would never get to the peak.

It was hot, unusually hot, and the children started following us, laughing, dancing. We got to the cliff top and the children left us. We stood looking out over an expanse of penetrating blue. Alone. We held each other. It was consuming, mystical.

After that I felt I wanted to stay awhile, find out what Greece means to me. I've got so many relatives here, so accommodation and food are free, and I'm going to teach English for spending money.

I miss you. It's just that I need to explore the country and myself, at least for this year. I've postponed my course until next year.

You have my address. Please write to me. I'm waiting for your news.

Love from your friend

Athena

She touches Athena's letter, smells the scent of her on the paper, imagines her bending over the letter with her hair brushing her arm as she writes. *I miss you Athena*. She takes pen and paper and starts to write.

Chapter 5

Tessa brushes her hair too quickly, pulling out knots, burbling to the mirror. 'I can't believe it. He's chosen me. Me! I've got to try to be clever. I'm so nervous.' She's one of ten students Professor Davids has selected to discuss their essays. Professor Davids is different to other lecturers who think undergraduates are stupid. He enjoys being a mentor for promising students, and ever since their confrontation in the tutorial, he's been interested in Tessa's work.

She rarely worries about clothes, but today she throws jumpers and skirts out of her cupboard. *No. No. I've got nothing to wear. Why do my parents care what I wear? Why can't they be like Athena's?*

She surveys her room with clothes piled everywhere and shakes her head. There are clothes on the floor, on her dresser, hanging halfway off hangers. *I just want ordinary jeans and a jumper.* She kicks a hanger. She's sick of looking like someone from another time and throws her black shoes against the wall.

The meeting is at three o'clock that afternoon. Tessa puts on her blue skirt and white top, and ties back her hair. She looks briefly in the mirror, then turns away disgusted, moving quickly to Peter's door.

She shouts as she knocks, 'Wake-up, Peter' and bangs her way down to the kitchen to the echoes of Peter's complaints. She mutters 'hello' to her mother and slams dishes onto the table, avoiding her mother's look. 'Sorry,' Tessa says, but she doesn't want to be sorry, guilty. Mrs Kassis is quiet as she boils the eggs for breakfast.

Mr Kassis already sits at the table. 'Tessa, your mother tells me you have a meeting with your English professor. You make us proud.' After she places the boiled eggs in front of him Mr Kassis takes her hands. *Papa, just leave me alone. You're choking me to death.* She pulls away.

Peter walks with Tessa to the bus stop. 'What's university like?'

'All right.'

That's no answer.'

'You don't care what I think.'

He smiles. 'Oh, it's about this morning, is it?' He shoves Tessa and she shoves him back. 'Can't a brother annoy his sister?'

'It's not about being a brother and sister. You just think you're so great, just because you're the male, the great man in the family.'

'You've got a real problem, Tessa.'

'Have I? Why don't you get up on time? Why don't you wake me up or get my breakfast?'

'Sure, Tessa.'

'Why should I tell you about university. I'm only there because Papa wants me to be worth more to a man, otherwise he'd just make me get married now. You'll be going there next year because it's your right.'

'You're in a rotten mood, Tessa.'

'I'm not. It just seems so unfair.' She looks down at her black shoes. 'Maybe you'll understand one day.' Tessa shrugs, looks at Peter who's kicking a stone along the footpath. She shakes her head, then starts talking about timetables and routines and buildings until the nothingness of the talk calms her. When she waves goodbye to Peter she's actually grateful.

The morning drags. She goes to a geography lecture with Jenny, which is mildly interesting, then studies in the library, which is tedious, and ends up watching a fly buzz around a half-eaten apple. Still two hours before her session with Professor Davids. She meets Jenny, who's on the way to 'The Pit'.

'What's that?'

'You know. It's where the student journal is. I've started working on it.'

'But you don't even like writing, Jenny.'

'You're funny. I'm not writing, I'm more important than that. 'Jenny slings her bag over her shoulder. 'I do layout and there are some cute guys there. Maybe you can write for the paper. Come on.'

'I don't think so.' Tessa follows Jenny. 'How do you know they want me there?'

'They need all the help they can get. They love free labour. The grant from the students' union only covers printing.' The wind catches Jenny's blonde hair. 'I'm thinking of getting my hair cut really short. What do you think?'

'No.' Tessa shakes her head. 'Your hair is beautiful. Don't you dare do that.'

'Well, we'll see. Anyway, you're coming with me now because I can't stand watching you for the next two hours, until you see Professor Davids. You've looked at your watch twenty-five times in the last ten minutes.'

'A slight exaggeration, I think.' Tessa follows her. They descend stairs that go into a dark hallway.

'There are no lights, Tessa. Just follow me.'

'Do you know where you're going?'

'Sure,' she laughs. 'It's the only place the student paper could get. No one else wanted this room.'

'I can see why.' There are more steps and Tessa trips.

'Are you all right?'

I'm fine.' Tessa trails behind Jenny. 'Do you know they've cut out the D. H. Lawrence elective?'

'I know. You 've told me about it quite a few times.' She shakes her head. Since Tessa has discovered D. H. Lawrence, she's been giving Jenny long lectures on *Sons and Lovers.* 'I'm sorry Tessa. I know you really wanted to do it.'

Tessa is quiet. *Sons and Lovers* wove disturbing patterns of human relationships, of love and obligation and the destructiveness between a parent and a child. She'd read horrified as the mother's love choked her eldest son and nearly destroyed the younger son. The D. H. Lawrence lectures had been cancelled. 'They put on another course that no one wants. Is it the money do you think? Or who's got the most power in the English faculty?'

Jenny shrugs. 'Well, if you were writing for the journal, you could investigate.' She stops. 'We're here. 'The Pit.'

There's arguing, typing, an Elvis Presley song coming from behind a door. Heads go up when they enter. There are hellos. Jenny introduces Tessa round, then starts to work on the layout of an article. *Abortion or the Pill*? 'Tessa, do you want to help?'

Tessa grimaces. Jenny moves the article around. Tessa shakes her head. 'It's wrong.'

'What? The pill, abortion, sex?' Jenny cuts out the heading to paste it at the top of the article.

Tessa shifts uncomfortably from one foot to the other. 'It's wrong. If you waited until you were married, then you wouldn't need the pill or an abortion.'

Jenny stands with her hands on her hips. 'Honestly, Tessa, so if you wait until you're married before sex. Afterwards, are you just supposed to have a baby every year?'

'I don't mean that. You can do other things when you're married.'

'Or not married.' Jenny shakes her head. 'Don't worry about it, Tessa. I think it's a good idea that you write for a different section. There's a creative writing insert in the journal. Try for that.'

Joel comes over to look at her layout. 'Great.' He playfully leans towards Jenny. 'Who's your beautiful friend?'

Only Athena calls her that. Makes her feel like that. Is he making fun of her? He winks at her. Tessa looks down at the floor.

Jenny rolls her eyes. 'Tessa meet Joel. He's the comedian here and marketing genius. He's going to make people want to read the journal.'

Tessa ends up photocopying, while she listens to jokes and conversations about boyfriends and demonstrations, arguments over the recession and unemployment. *I like this. I like this.* She suddenly shudders. *Papa wouldn't.*

At ten to three, she leaves for Professor Davids' rooms. At three exactly, she knocks on his door. 'Come in,' calls a voice from behind the door. Tessa hesitates.

'Come in.' The voice is louder, impatient. Professor Davids is at his desk writing. 'Just a minute.' He finishes, then puts down his pen. As usual, he looks untidy. His nose is prominent and his blue eyes deep-set. When he stands up, she smiles to herself because he does look a little like Heathcliff, except older. Thirty-one, according to the academic profile in the university gazette.

He takes out Tessa's essay, flipping pages quickly as if to remind himself. 'Oh yes, I found your interpretation of this work unusual.' He looks at her. 'That's good. You'll need more background here.' He discusses some of her arguments, then hands Tessa a list of questions and references. 'Ask yourself how far the poet is pushing the limits of definition. Read the references when you have a chance. Will you do the research? Will you ask the questions?'

Tessa knows him well enough to respond quickly. 'Yes, I will.'

He moves towards his shelves of books, taking out several references and handing them to her. 'Can you find new ways of answering old questions? Or are you going to just read the references and give them back to me in essays and pretend the ideas are yours?'

'I'm not a thief.'

'But we're all thieves of sorts. I take Coleridge's poetry and read it for all to admire me. Is it mine?'

'Yes, it's yours.' Tessa's heart pounds as she plays the game. 'It's the way you read it that makes it come alive.'

'You flatter my ego. I like that.' He laughs again. Tessa blushes. He ignores her embarrassment. 'And is Coleridge less than me, because I'm such a dramatic performer of his works?'

43

'Less? No. His poetry is unique. Your recitation is unique. It's different, that's all.'

'You barely scraped out of that one.' Suddenly he stops his intellectual game. 'I can see we're going to get on, Tessa.'

***

It's late when Tessa walks towards her front door. The house seems too big and she wants to run up to her room. She loves her shells and icon and the trees rustling outside her window, but it's very late.

Her mother stands nervously in the hallway. Tessa, you should have rung. We have worried. Your father is home from the factory.'

'Sorry. I'll explain to him.'

'And Tessa, you left your clothes lying everywhere in your room.'

'I'll put them away later, Mama.'

'I have done it.'

'I didn't want you to tidy my room.' Tessa raises her voice. 'It makes me feel awful when you do it. I'm responsible for my room. Can't you leave it alone?' Tessa wants to escape, but her mother takes her hand. She closes her eyes, promising herself. *I'll never be like you. Never.* Opening her eyes, she sees her mother standing watching her, a small anxious woman who serves, afraid. *But I love you.* She puts her arms around her. 'I've joined a student group who're doing a journal. I'll tell you about it and the professor.' Tessa kisses her. 'I'll speak to Papa first.' Her mother nods.

Mr Kassis is sitting in his usual armchair. He's a short, stocky man, but looks big. 'Well Tessa, what do you say?'

'I didn't know it was so late and the bus was caught in heavy traffic.' She feels she can't weave Athena's silken threads around his armchair. The professor kept me longer than I expected.' Tessa hopes there are enough excuses. I'm sorry, Papa.'

The professor? Yes, I remember.' Her father recalls. 'Did he like your work?'

Tessa sees she has the chance to weave a little, like Athena. 'Yes, he did. Papa, the professor showed me writing that made me understand literature and wonderful books. Books you would love.'

Mr Kassis wants to be angry, but he loves books and his daughter. He used to read stories slowly from the Greek myths at night to Tessa and Peter when they were small. He always knew that his little Tessa loved the stories best. She would ask him to read to her again and again, about the gods and goddesses who lived on Olympus.

She tells him about Professor Davids' rooms lined with aged classics bound in leather. 'There are books of Greek mythology, of Apollo, of Zeus, and poetry.'

He remembers. 'The only book my father had was the Bible. It was also covered in leather.' He nods at his daughter. 'I wanted to read it, but the words were complicated. I did read it in the end. The others were ignorant in the church, but not I.'

He speaks of the stories in his father's Bible. Tessa loves these times and feels the specialness of her father. Mr Kassis softens and it doesn't matter that dinner is late.

Chapter 6

Tessa is a Greek girl who helps her mother change the bed linen on Saturdays, and teaches Greek on Sundays in the small room attached to the church. She listens religiously to the doctrines of virginity, devotion to God, obedience, and the promise of eternal salvation. Tessa does as she is told and is rewarded by her parents' approval, her father's love, validation of her mother's life and a sense of safety and certainty.

At university, Tessa is a nineteen-year-old woman who helps produce the journal and is in a student group pressuring the English faculty for the reinstatement of the D. H. Lawrence course. She's part of the university community and listens to the student leaders argue politics and social justice. The rewards are being part of a larger world with friendships, growth, personal freedom.

Only rarely do the two worlds overlap.

***

Geography requires a two-day compulsory excursion. Tessa arranged to be sick on the two previous excursions, but now her tutor advises her that if she misses this excursion she'll fail Geography.

It's the weekend, and Tessa has planted some cuttings. She always marvels at the leaves emerging from small parts of plants. She wonders how she came out of her mother's womb and her father's sexuality. She shudders at the thought.

When Mr Kassis finishes mowing the lawn, Tessa runs to get him some water. He drinks thirstily, 'Good,' and hands her back the glass. She doesn't move back to her planting. 'Yes, Tessa?'

He can't be so ignorant that he won't let me go. Just be clever, like Athena. Manipulate him. 'Father, you know how you want me to do well at university?'

'Are you doing badly?' As he talks, he empties the cut grass from the tray of the mower onto the pile of compost.

'No.' Tessa hesitates. 'It's Geography. I have to do a soil study.'

'Yes?'

'That means going on an excursion.' She falters. 'It's two days, to the country.' She adds quickly. 'The lecturer will be there.'

Mr Kassis stops. He takes out his large handkerchief to wipe the sweat from his face. 'This is difficult. I have a duty to you.'

'Why? It's just an excursion. Everyone goes.'

'Yes, but you are not everyone. You are my daughter. ' He frowns. 'You will be alone, without protection.' Tessa tries to butt in but he shakes his hand. 'It is unsafe.' He pushes his handkerchief into his trouser pocket. 'I am sorry Tessa, but I cannot allow it. '

'Papa, please.'

He turns away from her, pushing the lawn-mower into the shed. Tessa stands silently watching him, but she's not silent in her mind. *You can't let me go, Papa? Why? Why? This is not your Greek village. What are you protecting me from? Against what? Do you think I'll sleep with a stranger on a night away? Do you think a man will seduce me? Rape me? Who would even want me?* She treads over the emerging plants and bends to touch the leaves. *I'm pure. Virginal. I've listened to the priest. Sex is a sin outside marriage.* Tessa strokes her arms, remembering Athena. *Papa, you don't have to worry, I won't waste myself on a furtive night in a cheap motel.*

Two days pass and Tessa withdraws. Her mother pleads. 'What's wrong?'

'Nothing.' Her mother's face is sad but Tessa won't speak to her. She wants to shake her mother. *You waited and were you saved?*

That evening Mr Kassis calls his daughter. 'I have thought a lot about this excursion. It is important. So, I have decided that you may go.'

Disbelievingly, she stares at her father, ashamed at her anger. Quietly she whispers, 'Thank you Papa.'

'I must know about this excursion.'

'Yes. There are information sheets. It's in three days.'

'That will be enough time. It will be an interesting trip. I like the earth of this country.'

'I do too.' She feels uneasy.

'We will have rooms that join. I will go with you. Joseph will manage the factory.' Mr Kassis walks away satisfied.

***

Tessa refuses to go to university, lying to her parents that there are no lectures. She retreats into her room, waiting for the excursion to arrive. She refuses to answer the phone when Jenny rings. She only comes down for meals. Over dinner Mr Kassis talks about the trip. 'You are fortunate to have such an opportunity. I always wished to study'

She stares at him. *I've got to say something. I just have to.* 'No one else's father is going.'

Mr Kassis tears bread from the freshly baked loaf. 'Well, I am different.'

Tessa feels like she's choking. 'But I'm not different.'

He puts down the bread. 'I am going for you, Tessa.'

She speaks slowly. 'You're not, Papa. It's not for me.'

'Tessa. Enough of this. It is organised.'

Tessa wants to scream at her father. *I hate you. I do. I do.* Mr Kassis enjoys the bread. Her mother brushes against her arm and Tessa looks up. Mrs Kassis whispers to Tessa, 'You have finished. Come and help me in the kitchen.' Tessa pushes away from the table and her father. Silently the two women wash and dry dishes together, until Mrs Kassis puts her hand on Tessa's arm. 'I understand, Tessa.'

'I don't want to go to university, or anything anymore.'

'Tessa, you must have choices in your life. I did not. I was very lucky that my parents choose your father for me when I was a girl.'

'I don't want anyone to choose my husband for me.'

'Please, listen to me Tessa.' Mrs Kassis gently pushes her daughter's hair away from her face. 'We married in the village and when your father came here and I was his wife, I could not speak the language. I had no family here, so I was afraid.' Mrs Kassis stacks the dishes in the cupboard. 'My island village was not a big city like Athens so I had little education. I have had no other life but here with your father and you children and I have been happy in this house.' She takes her daughter's hand. 'I want more for you.'

'He's ruining university for me. No one else's father would do it.' She blushes. 'It's humiliating.'

'He loves you. It is just your father's way. Please, I beg you, accept it.' Mrs Kassis kisses her daughter.

***

The excursion comes. Mr Kassis enjoys the study of landscape and soils. He speaks to the lecturer and the students, takes photographs of sandstone and clay, writes notes, makes observations. Some of the others taunt Tessa. 'Nice to have your daddy with you, isn't it? ' Others feels sorry for her. 'Look, it's fine really. Don't worry about it, Tessa.'

The bus speeds through the gnarled vineyards terraced between farmhouses and dams. It stops at a large winery where Tessa walks behind her father between the huge aluminium vats and the big oak barrels. They gather to listen to the winemaker explain the process. Afterwards Mr Kassis buys a very special chardonnay for home and a vintage red to share with the lecturer.

The bus stops at an open-cut coalmine with mounds of dirt piling black across the green fields. Tessa walks to the edge of the mine alone. She peers into the open cut that exposes layers of raw coal cut out of the land, into the land. *Is that me?* Glancing at Mr Kassis, Tessa shudders. He's standing with the other students listening to the lecturer explain the process that feeds coal into the huge electricity plants of the valley. *Is that me?* She looks away, only to see smoke belching into the air from tall stacks in the distance. The motel is in a small township with a traditional sandstone courthouse and sprawling pub. The students wander past the comer store and weatherboard schoolhouse to settle inside the pub. They don't ask Tessa and her father to join them.

Mr Kassis packs the white wine in his bag. He talks about the day unaware that Tessa is silent, hiding. *I'm not here, father. Don't you know that? You're talking to no one.*

On the bus trip home, Tessa watches the scenes pass lucerne grasslands, dairy cows with bloated udders, pink and grey galahs squawking in eucalyptus trees. *I'm not in the bus. I've disappeared. I can't hear them laughing at me, pitying me.* She withdraws until she's heart and lungs and veins. There are no ears or eyes or breath. She's at school again, but there's no Athena. Just her father.

The bus crawls back into Sydney. Mr Kassis shakes the lecturer's hand and leaves with anecdotes and memories. Tessa has memories too. She plans to drop Geography at the end of the year. For now, she avoids those students on the bus.

When Jenny asks her about her Geography trip, she is defensive. 'Why? Has anyone said anything?'

'Nothing. What is it?'

'Please don't ever mention the excursion to me.'

Other people ask, then stop. The excursion fades into that part of Tessa that is locked and hidden and she begins to skip Geography lectures.

***

Easter. The Kassis family regard the ritual seriously. The Pastoral Liturgy is observed on the first full moon after the Jewish Passover, but preparations begin long before the service. Tessa's glad of the Easter fast, forty days without meat, cheese, fish or butter. She wants to do penance to cleanse away anger at her father. She wants to show God that she's grateful for the gifts He's given her, the pleasure of studying literature, the love of Athena and Jenny, her family. Tessa laughs with her mother over gossip, as they carefully cook Easter spinach and cabbage and tomatoes. Afterwards they drink milk-less tea together.

There is a letter from Athena. Tessa savours her excitement, unfolding the letter slowly, spreading it out on her bed. She leaves the creamy paper and black ink to settle on the white sheets. Tessa takes out her Starry Moon shell and her icon and puts them next to the letter. She moves to the window, watching her trees waving in the breeze. Only when she senses Athena's presence does she settle on her bed to read.

Dearest Tessa

It was wonderful to receive your letter. I'm so glad you like university. I can't believe that you're working on a student paper.

Professor Davids sounds like he's worked out how talented you are. I'd really love to hear Professor Davids reading love poetry. I'm in love with everything here. My uncle's house in Athens is wonderful. It's a white flat building with windows opening to cool breezes.

It's hot here and the whiteness makes Athens glare. There's marble everywhere - broken pillars and parts of temples. I joined the hordes of tourists and climbed the Acropolis. I took a tiny piece of marble. There are signs everywhere that it's illegal to take it. I may have risked imprisonment, torture, death - but I still put it in my pocket. Now I have a piece of the Acropolis in my room.

I've stopped coaching English because I have a new job as a 'slave'. Maybe it's not quite a slave. I'm on a paper too. It's a daily Greek newspaper and I get to do exciting things like running around the office, taking sheets of paper from one desk to another. I'm working myself into a frenzy doing the midnight shift, but it's worth it. I'm getting experience and I've actually gone out with some of the journalists on important investigative reporting jobs. Well, maybe important is the wrong word. I had to follow up the case of the missing lion cub.

It was a bit stupid, so don't dare ask me why there was a lion cub here, and why it was missing and why it's news.

Maria Callas is always in the news. They say her voice has gone and so has her lover, Onassis, the richest man in the world. I'm not sure whether to be sad for her or not. Why did she waste her life on him? He's married as well. Is she immoral or just self-destructive? I don't know.

Anyway, back to the paper. It's crazy here. Greek politics are wild. Although I shouldn't say that after Australian politics. Is everyone still demonstrating against the governor-general or are they demonstrating against new things like uranium mining? I hate the thought of nuclear bombs, don't you?

I've developed a taste for ouzo. I didn't like it at first, the aniseed was a bit overpowering. But not anymore! Unfortunately for my cousin, I haven't developed a taste for him. He is in love with me.

I'm writing this in the newsroom, which accounts for the deterioration of the writing. Some of the journalists are getting loud. It's probably a murder or something. As you can guess, I'm needed. They want me to make coffee and bring the ouzo. It's my fatal flaw, being needed. Must go.

Love you

Athena

P.S. I'm going to a special Easter midnight service in the Acropolis. I wish I could share a candle with you there.

Dancing Queen sings from Tessa's radio. She lies on her bed holding Athena's letter. *Why have you gone away for so long? We've got things to share with each other.* Tessa imagines she's with Athena in her temple on top of the Acropolis.

***

University breaks for Easter holidays. Jenny's not going away. 'I've got too many assignments, unfortunately.'

'It's about time.' Tessa smiles. 'I'm looking forward to Easter services.'

'I'm not.' She digs in her bag. 'But I am looking forward to heaps of chocolate Easter eggs and pimples - yuk.' She grabs a package. 'Here's your egg.'

'Chocolate. My favourite health food.' Tessa unwraps the package. 'It's huge, Jenny. I'm going to get fatter.'

'You're not fat.'

'I don't know about that.' Tessa smiles. 'Here are yours. You won't get any pimples from these. They're traditional. I coloured them red for you. No chocolate in them.'

'Great. Less pimples and I like hard-boiled eggs.'

Tessa is curious. 'You are going to a service, aren't you?'

'No, I'm not.' She looks serious. 'You know, you can still believe and not go to church. I don't need a building and a minister.'

Tessa shakes her head. 'Easter's important. The church liturgies are part of it.'

'Then you should go. It's just not for me.' Jenny looks at the eggs. 'They're very red. I'm impressed.' She smiles. 'So, I'll see you after the holidays, Tessa.'

'Sure.' Tessa frowns.

'Don't worry. I'm not an atheist. I won't go to hell or anything.' Jenny puts her bag over her shoulder. 'Tessa, don't be so serious.'

'I'm sorry. Do all your assignments.'

Jenny laughs as she disappears down the path, her blonde hair catching the wind.

Every evening in the week before Easter Tessa goes with her family to the Greek Orthodox church. Peter walks beside his father. Tessa is reflective as the nightly observances move towards the crucifixion. Thursday night, the women chant plaintively the stations of the Cross. Mrs Kassis and Tessa chant. Incense, recitations of the nailing onto the wooden cross pervade Tessa's thoughts. She makes a decision to try not to question anymore, to be grateful for parents she respects and the affluence of her life. *I'm going to be the daughter they want, or at least try to be.*

Tessa dresses slowly on Good Friday. She puts on a black dress and joins her mother. Breakfast is meagre. They boil rice and some plain vegetables and leave them to cool on the kitchen table for later. Today is not for eating. There's just enough food to dampen the hunger pains.

The morning service is ritualistic, as the wooden frame is erected centre place in the Church, symbolising Christ's tomb. The men leave and the women commence decorating the tomb. Flowers lie profusely in bunches, waiting for them. Tessa joins hands with her mother in unravelling the whites of the orchids, gardenias, lilies. She immerses herself in the smell and touch of the flowers until she is aware of nothing but her senses. Intertwining flowers into the frame, she concentrates on the purity of the petals. The other women weave purple violets through the core of the tomb. The purple disturbs her. The violets are like violation, shocking the white with blood.

The priest in his black robe chants, marking the end of the decorating and the dedication by the women.

Tessa and her mother leave, exhausted. At home, her mother rests on the floral lounge. Tessa lies on her bed restlessly with the sheets pressing between her legs, with images of Athena between marble columns and her father standing like a colossus. It's dark when the Good Friday evening service starts. Mr and Mrs Kassis climb the steps of the church, followed quietly by Tessa and Peter. Tessa jumps, when she feels a heavy hand on her shoulder.

It's just a family friend, John Pappas, who wishes her a good Easter.

The worshippers gather solemnly. Tessa watches the old women in black and young girls in white who light candles in adoration of Jesus. The women pray before the statue of the man who is God, with his healing hands and beatific face. The three ritual chants lamenting Christ's death weave through the women and worshippers until Tessa feels encircled by them. Instinctively, she reaches out for Athena, spreading her hands, but it's only her mother who takes them.

The wooden, flower-covered tomb is lifted and carried through the church. Holding hands with her mother, Tessa follows the tomb as if in a funeral procession through the darkened streets with only lighted candles showing the way.

That night she sleeps deeply as the flowers of the church and the light of candles engulf her in the mystery of faith.

Easter Saturday means they can't even have water. Tessa watches her father with his head bent receiving Holy Communion. She knows he bends in confirmation of his beliefs. *I want to bend too.* The priest moves towards her with his silver chalice. *It's hard. Just don't think. Don't think.* Her stomach knots as the priest gives her wine and bread.

After the service, Tessa helps her mother prepare the feast that will break the Easter fast. Peter wanders into the kitchen to investigate the food, until Mrs Kassis slaps his hand. 'Out of the kitchen, you do not belong here.' Peter winks at Tessa. She grimaces.

'Okay, okay, I know when I'm not wanted.' He leaves them to join his father and the other men drinking black coffee and talking before the late-night service.

Humming, Mrs Kassis is renewed by fulfilling her duties as she cooks the special Easter offal soup. Tessa prepares the lamb for roasting. 'Don't you think Peter should help? I think he would.' Stirring the heart and lungs in the pot, Mrs Kassis shakes her head.

'Why is it always like this?'

Mrs Kassis wipes her hands on her apron. 'What do you mean?'

'We work and they eat. It's wrong. Can't you see it?'

'Please Tessa, I am content.'

Tessa presses her lips together. *I'm not content.*

At the 11 pm service, the church is crowded with cousins and friends and community. Mr Kassis sings determinedly, with Mrs Kassis and Peter following his lead. Tessa's voice wavers as lamentations unsettle incense and pews, rising into a crescendo of prayers. Then darkness, only darkness.

Midnight. A lighted candle flickers in the blackness. The priest's voice rejoices. 'Christ is risen.' The candle passes the light to another candle and the light is passed on until everyone is holding the light and the church blazes with light and singing.

The priest leads them down the aisle and into the night. Following behind him in a line of faith, the people celebrate in the streets the gift of redemption through Christ. Peter looks ahead but Tessa bends her head, watching the concrete slide under her feet.

Mr Kassis takes Mrs Kassis' hand and strides forward in belief. 'Christ is risen. Christ is risen.'

The early morning hours of Easter Sunday are filled with faith and family as they feast, cracking the red eggs representing life, salvation. Mrs Kassis carries the broken shells to the kitchen. Tessa follows her, taking the shells from her mother's hands.

Chapter 7

Easter ends and university days move quickly ahead. Tessa passes her first semester with a high distinction in English. Professor Davids approves. Her father is disappointed when she tells him she's changing Geography, to the terminating course for the next semester. He accepts it because he says 'English and Education are more important for your future.'

She has only ever touched success before. She'd win a third place in a running race or just miss out on a credit for history. It had never occurred to her to envy the winners because she wasn't meant to be a winner, that was all.

Tessa had clapped loudest when Athena received prizes. No one had ever clapped her, but they're clapping now. Parents, friends, the priest and Peter. 'Didn't know you were so smart, Tessa. You did a great job fooling me before,' Peter jokes. 'Just kidding. I expect serious help now with my English so I get into law next year.'

'Peter, are you sick or just desperate?'

'Desperate, of course.'

'Really?' Shaking her head, she thinks of the tedious chores she's done for her brother while he's kicked a football in the backyard or met his friends. Something he accepts because he's the son and because that's the way it's always been. Chores her father demands and her mother pleads with her to do, 'For your father, Tessa. For peace.' Looking at Peter closely, she knows he means it. 'Maybe I'll help you, but what do I get out of it?'

'Look at this smile on my face.'

'Yes?'

'My gratitude, Tessa. Gratitude.' Spreading out his arms, he bows to her. 'So, will you help me?'

'Maybe. Oh, all right.' They both burst out laughing.

***

It's Saturday morning and the phone rings. Tessa rarely gets calls, but it's for her. 'Jenny wants to speak to you, Tessa.' Mrs Kassis hovers while she picks up the phone.

'Have a great break, Tessa. I know mine will be. Wish you were coming with everyone.' Jenny's excited, speaking quickly, not expecting answers. 'Blue seas. Yellow sands. The Barrier Reef will be amazing and I'll get paid too. I just have the morning breakfast shifts. Then I'm free to play.'

Tessa keeps looking at her mother. *Jenny, hurry up. No, talk to me. Get off the phone. No, stay on the phone.* Shaking her head, she refuses to explain to Jenny about her parents. 'It shouldn't be too hot up there now, so you won't come back sunburnt.'

'Hope not, I can't stand pain. I wish I had your skin. You never burn. I've got to go. They're beeping the car horn. I'll tell you all about it when I'm back.

By the way, you'd better get your writing finished for the journal by then.'

'I will. So, I'll see you at university in a month.' Putting down the phone, she brushes past her mother. Just going to the garden.' Tessa doesn't wear gloves. She likes the dirt between her fingers. Her father has told her a hundred times that there could be red- back spiders, but he's not here now, so Tessa digs without them. She watches an earthworm burrow away from her fingers, then thinks about the other call she had yesterday from Professor Davids. It's so odd to have two phone calls. What does he want? Professor Davids had arranged a meeting for later that morning. Tessa brushes the dirt from her fingers and leaves the plants and soil.

***

Professor Davids walks out from behind his desk when Tessa enters his rooms. 'Sit down.' He leans against his desk looking down at her. She feels awkward but tries to look back confidently. *I'm not a schoolgirl anymore.* He asks her about her plans for the mid-break semester.

Tessa shakes her head. 'Nothing.'

They talk lightly about trivialities until he gets impatient and suddenly stops. Shoving papers to one side, he sits on his desk. 'Let's get to the point. Most students are away over the holidays partying or camping or whatever, but some of my honours students are helping me collect and collate some poetry research. Third- and fourth-year students mainly.' He adds quickly. 'Actually I pressured them.' He smiles. 'There has to be some advantage in being a professor. I need help. This part of the research has to be finished before classes begin. I've asked two other of my best first-year students to work on it. The question is, can you help me?' He looks at Tessa. 'I could say this is part of your course, but it isn't.' He laughs. 'You see, I'm not a thief or a liar.' Tessa smiles at the private joke between them. 'Will you help me? I'm fairly desperate.

It's unpaid of course.' He waits for a second. 'I promise you won't be penalised if you can't assist me.'

Tessa looks down at her hands. The nails are bitten and chewed. *What if I say no? He'll lose interest in my work. I suppose it'll help me if I do it. It'll be an excuse to escape. I won't have to visit the relatives. I won't have to help my mother clean.* 'Yes.'

He pushes himself off his desk, grinning. 'Come on then, Tessa. To work.' Tessa follows him into an adjoining room where three students are engrossed in piles of papers and books. They look up as he enters and he introduces Tessa. 'You'll show her what to do, won't you?'.

The older student pretends to groan. 'There's plenty to show.'

Professor Davids quips back. 'It's building up your stamina. Think of it as gymnastics for your doctorates. It's muscle-building, except not for the body, for the mind.' He looks at Tessa. 'You'll have to do some reference work in the library as well. It'll be good experience, help your research skills.' Tessa smiles at his manipulation. 'Can you start now?'

'Yes,' she answers quickly.

'Excellent. Then I'll leave you here.' Tessa bites her lip. 'I'll be back at lunchtime.'

She is acknowledged briefly. The older student waves her over. 'Just follow me. Shelley there and Keats there and so on. Don't worry, you'll get into it.' Tessa is awkward as she copies him, conscious that she's the youngest one and the least experienced. She reads the documents carefully before classifying them, asking a question only when she's really unsure. Then she's directed to another pile. 'The best part of this job is lunchtime with him, except he doesn't always make it. He'll come today because you're new.' The door opens. 'One-thirty. Are you starving yet?' Professor Davids calls out to them. Tessa looks up. 'Come on, then.' She'd forgotten about time and food.

They leave the papers to follow the professor like the mice of Hamlyn.

The university is deserted in the vacation period except for a few keen academics and a skeleton staff of employees. As they leave the stuffy rooms, the winter air feels sharp. Tessa pulls her jumper around her shoulders. They walk past halls and sandstone buildings, that are being extended with concrete and aluminium. Tessa kicks gravel to the side. She hates the changes. Her education lectures are in those modern buildings with television monitors overhead and laminex desktops. You can't even initial boredom into the wood.

Professor Davids leads the students past other buildings, with gothic gargoyles staring from the top of rising bell towers. They wind through gardens of Wandering Jew growing purple along grassy slopes, past old dirt tennis courts. They avoid the new artificial green courts next to the Science Block.

Professor Davids enjoys himself, reciting lines from Shakespeare as they follow, Pied Piper-like. Tessa trips on the roots of an old oak tree and falls behind. She has to run to catch up and arrives panting as Professor Davids flings a tartan picnic rug over the grass.

They're in a garden secreted behind overgrown trees and bush. He lays long French loaves, cheese and small tomatoes. out on the rug. They tear the bread roughly with cold hands. Tessa jumps as images of her father's ordered table cross the tartan rug. She shakes the images out of her head. *You're not welcome here, Papa. Disappear.* She giggles as he vanishes in a puff.

The students call the professor David. It amuses him. 'You call me David too, Tessa' he demands. 'I like the name David, the name of the Old Testament king. Michelangelo's David. Have any of you been to Italy?' No one had. 'Michelangelo's statue is impressive, huge, with marble hands and feet and a body that look like they could control the world. David was a conqueror, but he was only a boy when he flung his stone against the giant Philistine. Let's hope there are some fighters here.' Tessa doesn't disturb the talk. She listens intently to the older students discussing their work with I Professor Davids as he plays, throwing words and I ideas against them, forcing new answers, new thoughts. Suddenly he turns his attention to Tessa.

'*Tiger! Tiger! burning bright.*' Now, Tessa, '*What immortal hand or eye could frame thy fearful symmetry?* Are you afraid?'

She answers nervously. 'Yes, I'm afraid.'

'That's fair.'

'But I'm not afraid of the tiger.'

'He can tear you apart, Tessa.'

'Yes, but only my body, not my soul. It's only the man inside me that can tear my soul apart.'

'I can see you'll appreciate Blake. I will lend you my Blake's *Songs of Innocence and Experience*.'

Abruptly Professor Davids ends the picnic. They leave the garden to walk in different directions. There'll be other occasions with him.

***

Tessa goes every day to the university. Her father is proud that the English professor values his daughter's work, but her mother is lonely. Mrs Kassis looks forward to the holidays when Tessa chats and sings and gardens, but she doesn't complain when Tessa leaves for university. Tessa refuses to look at her mother. *I can't give this up, even for you, but I'll make it up.*

She works with her mother in the late afternoons and on the weekends. At night, she seeks out her father and listens to his stories. She helps Peter with his essays and he's actually grateful. She does her duties uncomplainingly. The house eases under Tessa's change.

The other students work for Professor Davids for one or two weeks or for a few days here and there. Tessa goes every day, until a natural familiarity develops between them.

One of the students teases her about it. 'I think you like more than Professor Davids' research.'

'Don't be ridiculous.' Tessa busies herself with papers so that he can't see her embarrassment.

Sometimes David and Tessa drink coffee together in his rooms. He likes his coffee strong, like her father does. She no longer has adolescent dreams about Professor Davids being a Heathcliff. He's too real.

Sometimes he shocks her with his revelations of university politics, with its lobbying for funds and control. She talks to him about the D. H. Lawrence course. He's cynical. 'There will be funding when the right person sits on the university board.' Tessa has sensed the politics before but doesn't want to understand his cynicism. She argues that university is still a place where students can think freely, where there is an opportunity to study without restrictions. That makes Professor Davids laugh. 'You're an innocent, Tessa.'

Sometimes he's exhausted from the pace he works at. Then he likes to put away his research and university matters. 'What do you do outside these rooms, Tessa?'

'Nothing.'

'Now that's a challenge. Do you do nothing when you get up, and nothing with your family? Are you doing nothing every weekend, when you're not here?' He enjoys his sarcasm. He pauses a minute for effect. 'Do you know, I hate nothing answers.' Tessa is silent. He expects a clever retort and is irritated when she looks away. 'Answer me.' Tessa frowns, pressing her lips together. 'Are you angry?' She doesn't answer. 'I think you are.'

She bites her lip. 'What I think... ' She doesn't finish her sentence. She feels he's taunting her, ordering her. She won't accept his orders, not here, in the old university rooms.

'What have I done to make you so angry, little girl?' He's amused.

'I'm a woman.' She stares at him defiantly. 'And I won't be told what to say, when to answer you.'

He's surprised. 'Tessa, I didn't mean to tell you. It's just a game. Are you upset?' He lowers his voice. 'I'm sorry. Really, I am sorry.'

'I'm not upset.' She looks down. She doesn't tell him there are only orders and demands in her home. That the father she loves, is overpowering. That she obeys.

She doesn't want to. 'Maybe we're not friends, but I have a right to be treated as a person with equal rights. You have to ask me, not tell me.'

'I hope we're friends, Tessa.'

Tessa nods uncertainly, unsure if she has misunderstood, unsure whether she's been the offender or he. They talk a little more and, as a peace offering, he tells her how his father introduced him to literature. Professor Davids leans against the window ledge, framing himself in oak. 'My father read the European poets, but I remember his amazement when he discovered John Keats. *Beauty is truth, truth beauty - that I? all ye know on earth, and all ye need to know.* He found that profound. I was glad that he passed it on to me.'

'Was your father an academic too?'

He shakes his head. 'My father came here after the communist revolution in Hungary in 1956. He couldn't speak English then and no one could speak Hungarian.' He smiles. 'It's not the most common language in the world. Now. Greek is more useful.'

'What did your father do?'

'He was a builder. He liked that. It seemed something substantial to do.'

'My father makes furniture.'

That's substantial too, Tessa.' He turns to look out of the window and watch people stroll into the Great Hall with violins and cellos. There's a recital this afternoon. My father enjoyed Mozart and Strauss. I took him to some of the recitals in the Great Hall.' He reflects. 'He loved the intellectual life and that's what he shared with me after dinner, in the evening. But he died several years ago.'

'I'm sorry.' Tessa pauses. 'Did he like living here?'

'Migration's hard. You lose your roots. Miss it. But there wasn't anything left in Hungary for him. He was grateful to be here.'

'Tessa hesitates before she speaks. 'My father. Well, he's never really adjusted to the way we live in Australia, but he's Australian. He's not an intellectual, except he likes learning.'

'That's important, Tessa.' He pauses. 'So, are we friends now?'

She nods.

***

Tessa can't believe that a month's gone and Jenny's back from her trip up north. She's sunburnt when she meets Tessa in the cafeteria. 'Told you I needed your olive skin.' Jenny's excited. 'We did everything.'

'I can make great toast now.' Jenny speaks in a high pitched polite tone. 'Would you like marmalade or strawberry jam? Oh, you'd like yellow pumpkin jam? I'll see what I can do. I'll be back in a jiffy, just have to pull out a few pumpkins from the garden first.' They both laugh.

'Well, I have plenty of pumpkins in the garden if you need any.'

'Thanks so much, Tessa. I'll just give that a miss. It was terrific. We danced every night. I went on midnight swims. The water was warm there. The best days were our days off. There are deserted beaches only about fifteen minutes' walk from the hotel.' Her blue eyes flash. 'I met a fabulous guy. We did heaps of trekking.

None of the tourists could be bothered. I collected some old pieces of broken coral and shells. I know you love shells and brought you back this one. It looks like a tortoise.'

Jenny hands Tessa a package. She carefully unwraps the paper and feels the smooth, honey-flecked cowrie shell with its narrow opening. She rubs her fingers against the rough edges of the opening which guards the pinkie white insides. The shell feels cool. Tessa puts it against her ear. 'It's the sea. I love it, Jenny.'

'Maybe next time you can come with me?'

'Maybe.' Tessa hates the lie. Keats' words repeat in her mind. *Truth. I want to tell the truth.* She doesn't want to evade, to pretend anymore, not to Jenny. 'I wish.' She coughs. 'Jenny, I can't ever go with you. I want to, but I don't even try to think about it.' Tessa hesitates because she feels like she's betraying her father and mother. 'My parents wouldn't let me go.' She rubs her hands. 'It's because they can't understand that it's different to when they were growing up. They have to keep me safe.'

'Safe from what?'

'Everything. The world.' Tessa pretends to laugh.

'Athena's parents aren't so protective, but my parents still think they're in the villages they came from.' Tessa bites her nail. 'I feel guilty telling you.' Tessa looks at her friend. 'There've been things I haven't told you.' She speaks slowly. 'The Geography excursion. I know you didn't understand.' Tessa breathes deeply. 'There are things I've kept secret that I want to tell you about school and my family and coming from where I do. Do you want to hear?'

'Of course.' Jenny listens as Tessa tells her about duties and obligations, about religious doctrine and family pressure.

When Tessa finishes, Jenny whispers, 'It's okay.'

'I don't have to make any more excuses to you now about why I can't go' to a play, or a party, or a trip.' Tessa hesitates. 'Are we still friends? '

'Always, Tessa.

Chapter 8

The university term starts and Professor Davids thanks his honours students, with an afternoon party in his rooms. He's exuberant with the completion of the first section of his work and pours poetry into conversations and drinks. Dramatically he recites *The Lady of Shalott*.

On either side the river lie
Long fields of barley and of rye,
That clothe the wold and meet the sky;
And thro' the field the road runs by
To many-tower'd Camelot;
...
Round an island there below,
The island of Shalott.

The verses of Tennyson and Shakespeare and whatever comes into the student's minds, create a river of words, rhyming into laughter and romance and death, floating in a boat down to Camelot. Drinking, singing, they bang away to verses that become crazier as they fall into the professor's mood. Tessa recites:

She floated down to Camelot
And as the boat-head wound along
The willowy hills and fields among,
They heard her singing her last song,
The Lady of Shalott.

She drinks her fourth glass of wine. People start dancing and someone drags Tessa into the circle. She swirls around and around until she's dizzy, twirling uncontrolled. David catches her in a pirouette and the two of them fall onto a couch. 'Too much wine for this

71

Greek girl.' Tessa doesn't argue. She closes her eyes. 'I think you're going to have a big headache tomorrow.'

'I don't feel very well.'

Professor Davids drives her home. She whispers, 'I've never done this before.'

'You're doing what all students do eventually. Red wine and I have had a few bad nights.'

Tessa can see her home at the end of the road. 'Please, could you stop here,' she whispers even more quietly. 'My father wouldn't accept this. I don't think I do either.'

He parks a little before her house so that no one sees and helps her out of the car. 'It's all right Tessa, I understand.' She wonders if he does. If he realises that her father would be angry that a man, even her professor, has driven her home. She'll lie about David and the party and too much wine and she feels ugly inside.

Her father is waiting for her as she enters the house. 'Where have you been? What is wrong with you?'

He interrogates her until she begs him to stop. 'I'm sick, Father. Let me go to my bedroom. Please.'

He shakes his head because he is never sick and never misses work, is never late for church or the events of life. 'Then you had better go to your bed. We will talk another time.' He pauses. 'Are you late because you are sick? Is that correct?'

'Yes, Papa.'

He's tender then and strokes her face. 'Go and sleep.' Her mother follows her up the stairs worrying, bringing lemon water and toast to her room. Tessa lets her fuss, plumping up the pillow, tucking in the doona. She feels protected and suffocated, like a schoolgirl again. She burrows into her bed.

It takes a whole day for her headache to go. Mr Kassis asks if she is better the next morning over breakfast. Mrs Kassis makes her sweet tea. Even Peter is kind, and places his plates carefully on the table so as not to make too much noise. That makes Tessa laugh, which hurts her head. She presses her hands over her forehead. 'Peter, I think you've definitely improved.'

By the afternoon, she feels better. She reads through her article, that argues for the reintroduction of the D. H. Lawrence elective. Then she looks through her papers. She's always written for herself describing the trees outside her room, her feelings for Athena, the smells of incense in church, her fantasies, the rough hands of her father's boyhood. Lately her writing has taken more form because of her studies at university and the research for Professor Davids. The journal committee has asked her to submit some work for the creative writing section.

Ruffling through her scribblings she reads a few pieces, then shuffles them back into the desk drawer. Scared. *What if they think, I can't write? That this is hopeless or, even worse, ordinary. I don't want to be ordinary anymore. I just don't.*

The second day Tessa's headache is gone. She meets Jenny on the front lawn after morning lectures. Tessa is nervous. 'Jenny, I really need your advice.'

She hands Jenny two of her poems. 'You've got to tell me the truth,' Tessa says, 'even if it hurts.'

Jenny puts her hands on her hips. 'Okay. This must be serious stuff.'

73

'Maybe I shouldn't... '
'Shush, let me read.'

The Teacher
I want to make an impression.
I want them to admire.
But they see
a woman
fifty-four
spreading into
grey skirt and pleated
blouse
plastic lensed frame
on her nose.
They dismiss the middle-aged woman.
'Look at me,' I scream in my head.

I have passion.
I run along beaches
 throwing sand in the air
stripping pleats to stand naked
with blue water washing my thighs.
I nod,
my head bobbing like a doll
hard, white, rigid
and they say 'devoted to her profession'
'good teacher, but unimaginative'.
LIES
LIES

Jenny looks questioningly. 'Is this a trick? It's not about you, unless you're fifty-four. You're not middle-aged.'

Tessa shakes her head. 'It is me. I wear a grey skirt and pleated blouse.' Jenny raises her eyebrows. 'Don't look like that.'

'All right, explain it.'

'Have you ever felt trapped?'

'Sometimes.'

'This is about being trapped by how you're supposed to behave. Trapped by a role, like being a teacher or a mother, or by your age, like being fifty-four or nineteen. Trapped by everyone's expectations and judgments.' She waits. 'There has to be more inside a. person. If people really looked, they could find someone exciting or someone who at least has a different vision.'

'Like you, Tessa.' Jenny reads the second poem Tessa's given her, 'Rites'. She hands them back. 'Give them to the journal committee. I don't know if they'll publish them, but you've got to risk it.'

'I suppose. I've got to be brave.' *Like Athena.*

***

Tessa loves literature. Sometimes she walks with the other students and Professor Davids after a tutorial, discussing Shelley or Keats. When he asks, she still helps the research students with David's work. She used to enjoy being with them, listening to their arguments over books and the university and the gossip of lives that are different to hers, but lately their comments have hurt her. 'Maybe you should rub David's shoulders for him this afternoon, Tessa. He works so hard.' 'Only love poetry for you. I'll get the religious poems instead,' they tease her. *They're jealous, that's all. I'll ignore them.* But she avoids them instead, going to help

Professor Davids when they're not there, like this afternoon.

Tessa files his papers for a while before disturbing him at his desk. Sometimes he's angry when she does that, but today he just looks up questioning. She's uncomfortable. 'I hope you don't mind?' She stammers and mumbles until he grins.

'Come on, what is it?'

'Will you read this poem? I want to submit it to the journal, if it's good enough.' He pushes away his books and takes the poem from her hands.

Rites

an ordinary village resting on crags

between two other villages and a dirt road.

ordinary people praying for journeys between dawn and a man's work.

For food soil tilled tradition woven into

the wedding dance and continuation.

'We have something in common, Tessa.' He re-reads the poem, 'Did you write this for me?' Tessa's confused. He smiles. 'I know you didn't. It's your family, your tradition, isn't it?' She nods. 'I grew up with similar traditions.' He presses his fingers against the words 'lighting candles'. 'Every year when I was a boy, I'd watch my father light a candle for eight days until nine candles burned. It's an ancient tradition, like your traditions, Tessa. You know, Jews today celebrate this miracle from God where a light burned without oil many thousands of years ago in the Tempie of Jerusalem. They call it the *Festival of Lights*, Hanukkah.' Professor Davids rubs the knuckles on his wiry hands.

'My mother's not Jewish, and since my father died we don't celebrate the *Festival of Lights* in my family anymore. I miss the tradition.'

Tessa nods, because she knows about her Greek Orthodox candles, lit for services and prayer before icons and saints. Tessa tells Professor Davids about her family, the villages of her parents, the traditions of the past, the rituals of work and responsibility. She pushes back her black hair. 'I've told my father about your leather-covered books.'

He smiles. 'My father taught me that books are a way to learning and learning is the one thing that no one can take away from you.' He strokes his black moustache with his thumb. 'Books are more than that of course. They are a gateway to understanding.' He pauses. 'Well, Tessa. I like your poem. We'd better get back to work.' David watches Tessa for a while, as she collects books to put back into the shelves. She concentrates, stretching her arms up to the top shelf. As she turns to collect more from the desk, he notices the top of her blouse has opened a little, exposing the soft line of her breasts. He shakes his head. Definitely off limits. Too young and Greek and there are the restrictions of her culture. He thinks of the girls from his father 's culture, hidden behind head shawls and long dresses, waiting for marriage and continuation.

***

Tessa spends increasing amounts of time in The Pit. The first edition of the journal has just been completed and they are working on the second, but it's become more than the work place for the journal. Students meet for creative writing groups. Others drop in to socialise. The students drink too much coffee, smoke cigarettes and dope while others shout at them to 'put it out'. Tessa listens to arguments over contraception, unemployment, the proposed anti-discrimination laws.

'If there are equal rights for women, who 'll make the coffee?' Joel calls out.

'Not me!' Carole shouts back. The world seems bigger here.

Tessa flicks through the first edition of the journal, to discover her poetry printed in the New Writing section. She catches her breath when she sees it. They hadn't told her.

Jenny arrives with a huge poster. 'Save the Refuge'. Tessa, they're threatening to cut funding, can you believe that? Jenny drops the poster with a crash onto a desk. 'You've got to come to the solidarity meeting at lunchtime. If the refuge is closed, those women and children will have nowhere to go.'

'Sure, I'll come.' Tessa doesn't show Jenny her poetry. It seems trivial when compared to the refuge. Tony's meeting me there. He'll be a great social worker when he finishes his degree, don't you think?'

No, I don't. 'Yes, he'll be great.' Tessa doesn't like Tony. She's not sure if it's because he's such a know-all, always telling everyone what they should think about unemployment, music, the refuge, or if it's because she's jealous. It's been hard since Jenny's met him. She's always busy these days playing squash at lunchtime with Tony, or meeting Tony at the pictures after classes, studying with Tony.

Jenny crashes into a few people with her poster, as they navigate steps and corridors to get out of the pit.

Tony waves when he sees them. He's nearly as noticeable as Jenny's poster with his reddish hair and two-metre frame. The demonstration is noisy, but it's Tony's comments on the plight of abused women and children that annoy Tessa. Just shut-up, Tessa wants to scream at him. She moves to Jenny's other side. 'What do you see in him Jenny? You have no opinions when he's around.' Tessa stands close to Jenny. She notices Tony's arm is around Jenny's waist. The demonstration ends with a pledge to lobby the government for more funds. Tessa walks quickly away from them to Professor Davids' rooms. She has an essay to collect.

'Another, high distinction. You're becoming my star student. Or are you just a star? You've got so many bright ideas.' David grimaces. 'My jokes are awful lately. I must be tired.'

'You still make me laugh.'

'Old joke, Tessa. You're a rising star. It's better than being a falling star.' Handing her back the essay, he's reflective. 'I don't have to catch you anymore.'

Tessa takes out her copy of the journal. 'Can I show you this?' She won't show her parents. They'd be shocked seeing obscenity in the photo of a naked girl on the front cover, blasphemy in other ways of seeing God, immorality in the sexuality, profanity when 'bloody ' is just that.

'Congratulations, Tessa.'

'It means a lot to me that.' She blushes. 'That I can share it with someone.'

***

After dinner Tessa sits at her desk reading the journal, when there's a knock on her door. She quickly

79

hides it under some books. It's Peter. She's surprised. Peter rarely comes to her room. He has a journal in his hand. 'Some students were giving these out on the street and guess whose name was inside.' He plonks himself down on the bed. 'Not bad,' he says. 'I don't know what the parents would think, though.'

Tessa moves pens and paper scattered on her desk. She's been closer to her brother lately, less angry at his casual acceptance of his male position in the family. It's not his fault. They've talked more since she's been at university and he's gone with her to some events.

The poem Rites made me think of our father.' He holds Tessa's journal with the pages open to her poems.

'I love writing.' Tessa bites her nail. 'I wish I could just write.' She sits next to Peter on the bed. 'I don't want to be in a library listing books, even if I love what's written inside them. Even if I respect librarians. The gateway to my books.'

'You probably won't even work when you 're married.'

'Married? Peter, that's pathetic. Haven't you heard that marriage isn't everything?'

'Sure, sure.'

Tessa throws a pillow at him.

'Okay, okay. Write then.'

'But I can't tell Mama or Papa. It'll be like lying to them. I hate that.'

Peter moves uncomfortably. 'Why can't you just be glad you're. at university? Not everyone gets the chance.'

'Athena's parents wouldn't force her to do what she didn't want to do.'

'They're different. Anyway, what's the point of talking about other families?'

'I want to write full-time. I want to do that for a job. Is that so selfish? You can do what you want, Peter.'

'I can't, you know.' He hesitates because he's not used to talking seriously to his sister, or anyone. 'It's just that I want what Papae wants to study law. There's no conflict.' He looks at Tessa. 'Why don't you keep quiet about it and write when you can? It's easier that way. You'll have to anyway in the end.'

Tessa doesn't answer. She stands up from the bed and moves to the window. *Maybe I'm selfish. I wish I could just accept it.* The breeze rustles the leaves.

'You know the pressure is pretty tough at school. I have to get really high marks to get into Law.'

She turns to Peter. The wind blows through her hair, catching strands on her lips. She brushes them aside. 'You'll do it.'

'I have to. It's harder than I thought.' He pauses. 'But if I make it into law, I'm doing international law.'

'You'd look great in a pinstriped suit and dark glasses running to catch a plane to New York. Or would you prefer Paris?'

'Paris. That's my style. The real me.'

'Except you'll have to take Mama along. Who'd iron your shirts and wash your socks?'

'Have you ever heard of the laundry?' He laughs. 'Not as good as her, but okay.'

'Really, will you be happy doing law?'

'Yes. I will.'

Tessa listens quietly as he talks about his plans for the future, and dreams that are different to hers.

81

Peter gets up from the bed. 'I think it's great about the journal.' He kisses his sister before he starts to leave.

'I'm glad you're doing what you want. You'll be the greatest lawyer.'

Afterwards, Tessa leans against the door enjoying the bond between her brother and herself. *We're connected, Peter. We're connected. You'll never tell them, will you?*

Chapter 9

Tessa joins the creative writing meetings. The back room of The Pit is recognised as the writers' group alone and a sign, 'Creative geniuses at work', has been glued to the door. They read their work to each other there. Only the committed come because there's a ruthlessness in the criticism. Egos are broken down, sometimes rebuilt and sometimes not. The weak leave. Soon there's only a core of four. Tessa, Joel, Carol and Jenny when she's not with Tony. Tessa loves the creativity, which is outrageous, obsessive. Sometimes they read the works of poets and other writers who inspire them, works Professor Davids touches on in lectures.

Tessa writes poetry late into the night, when it's so dark that the movements of the trees outside seem like strangers breaking in.

Her literature essay is late, so she brings bribes to appease Professor Davids. 'My mother and I made these biscuits for you over the weekend, so I couldn't finish my essay on time. Here it is now.'

He's amused. She hands him the plate of biscuits. 'I suspect we're becoming a little familiar here Tessa. Are you abusing my good nature?'

'Never. Just try the almond ones.' He takes one and Tessa hands him her essay. 'Can I give you some of my other writing too? The biscuits are delicious, aren't they? ' She blows sweet powder over her work.

'You're grubby, Tessa.' He flicks the sugar away. 'I'll accept it being late this time. Don't do it too often.' He puts aside the essay and looks at her creative writing and wonders if she knows how much she's exposing herself.

She leaves Professor Davids rooms to meet Jenny in the library. They haven't seen each other very much lately because of Tony. Heading for the talking room, they catch up on news. 'I've finally persuaded Peter to come to a poetry lecture.'

'That could be a mistake,' Jenny laughs. 'You said you were getting on better with him. Don't you think this could set things back a bit?'

'Very funny. Poetry is good for the soul and he needs it. The lecture is on at the end of the week. Do you want to come?'

'I think I'll give it a miss.'

They drop their books on a table, then spread out paper and pens and texts. Jenny scribbles down notes, copying from Tessa's notebook and talking at the same time. 'I went away camping with Tony last weekend, in the Blue Mountains. Just fantastic. I love the cliffs and smell of eucalyptus, don't you?'

'Yes, except I don't get to go very much.' Tessa's curious. 'Don't your parents mind that you go away with Tony?'

'No, they 're fine about it. Mum's busy. She's always working out new training programs at the bank. She just got her third promotion. We celebrated it at the local Chinese restaurant last night. 'Jenny stops writing for a second. 'I think Dad finds it all a bit hard. Mum's making more money than he does driving a truck.'

'My father would just hate that. He has to be in control of everything.'

'It's stupid, really.' Jenny bites the top of her pen. 'Anyway, my parents think I'm old enough to make my own decisions. I'm independent,' she smiles. 'Well, nearly. I'm lucky Mum and Dad don't expect me to pay board. I only have to pay for clothes and things like that.'

'Board? My father would never take money from me. I've some saved from Christmas and birthday money,' Tessa opens her reference book 'but it's not enough to live on, and I'd never be allowed to work anyway, so I guess I'll always be dependent.'

'Doesn't that bother you?' Jenny puts down her pen. 'Finished that section.'

'Of course, it does, but there's not much I can do about it, without starting a major revolution.' Tessa bites her nails. Freedom at university is fragile. Her father always seems to hover over it. Jenny hits Tessa's hands. 'No biting your nails. I thought you gave that up.'

'Well, I've improved. Does that count?'

Jenny shakes her head, then tells her about her mountain weekend. Swimming in mountain streams, walking around big old gum trees, getting a flat tyre in Tony's old bomb of a car.

'I miss talking like this, Jenny.'

'Me too.' They promise to see each other after lectures most days, even if Tony is in Jenny's life.

The afternoon of the poetry lecture arrives. The topic is *The Relevance of Shakespearian Love Poetry Today'*. Peter whinged about it all week but he's standing in the quadrangle now waiting for Tessa. This had better be good. You know I've taken off time from studying for it.'

'It 'll be great. I helped you with your Macbeth, didn't I? All you have to do in return is come here and be inspired.'

'Sure, sure.'

As they enter the lecture hall, they see Professor Davids already on the podium, so they quietly sneak into a back seat. He's arguing the case for Shakespearian love sonnets. Peter starts to fidget, tapping his fingers on the wooden bench. Then he starts to move from one side of the bench to the other trying to get comfortable. When he gives a gigantic yawn, Tessa elbows him in the ribs. 'Ouch. That hurt. Let's go, Tessa.' She ignores him. 'Come on,' he whispers in her ear. 'Who'd really say to a girl, *Shall I compare thee to a summer's day*?'

'You're so unromantic. Just be quiet and listen. You might learn something.' They stay until the end of the lecture, because it's too difficult to leave without disturbing other students.

'The end. Thank God. He's a real candidate for paper airplanes. I wish I had some paper to throw one at him. That was worse than death.'

'It wasn't. I loved it, except for you.' She walks away.

Peter runs after her. 'Wait, Tessa. Can' t you take a bit of honest criticism?'

She groans.

'Okay, okay. Maybe love poetry just isn't my greatest interest. You should be happy that I tried to listen.' He looks at his watch. 'Are you coming home now?'

'No. I'm sorry you hated it.'

'Don't worry about it.'

'I'm meeting Jenny.'

'Okay. Then I'm going home to study.' Peter brightens up. 'And you owe me another essay after this.'

'Sure, Peter.'

He races off to catch the bus.

***

Jenny's sitting on the sandstone fence on the front lawn. She waves half-heartedly. Tessa jumps onto the fence next to her, rattling on about Peter and Professor Davids' lecture.

Jenny's uninterested. She jumps off the sandstone fence, grazing her legs a little. 'Ouch.' She rubs the sore spot.

'Are you okay?'

'Fine,' Jenny grunts. She doesn't look at Tessa. 'The trouble with you is that you put Professor Davids on a pedestal. He's all right but I like my tutor better. He corrects my sentences and helps me with reference lists.'

'Are you annoyed?' Tessa watches her digging the tip of her shoe into the grass.

'I'm not annoyed. I feel a bit sick that's all.' Tessa teases, remembering her red wine afternoon.

'Too many parties, Jenny?'

' No. Don 't be stupid. '

Tessa's surprised. 'Sorry. Are you angry at me for something? '

'Tessa, I feel awful, that's all.'

'Can I do something to help?'

'You can't help.' Jenny shakes her head. 'Just go away.'

Tessa stands up, but she doesn't move away. She puts a hand on Jenny's shoulder. 'What's wrong?' Tessa waits, watching her. Jenny's hardly audible. 'Something.'

'Is it Tony?'

'Yes,' she whispers, 'and me.'

Tessa glances at the poster of bra-less girls in T-shirts on the library wall, and students lying together half hidden under trees. Sexuality seeps between lawns and lectures, challenging her home. 'Have you…'. Tessa leaves the question uncompleted because it's a sin. The priest, her father, her mother say it's a sin.

Jenny shakes her head. 'It's not that, Tessa.'

'Please tell me. Maybe I can help.'

She focuses on Tessa. 'Help? I wish you could.'

'Trust me, Jenny.'.

Taking a deep breath, she blurts out. 'I'm pregnant. Two months.' Jenny bends her head, so that her blonde hair partially covers her face. 'You don't even know what it's about do you?'

'Oh Jenny,' Tessa whispers.

Jenny's crying. Tessa has half read books on sexuality and seen the spreading bodies of the wives of her cousins. She watches Jenny and thinks of the lighted candles in her church and the forbidding black robes of priests and men and the sin.

'You hate me, don't you?'

'Hate you?' Tessa repeats. 'I could never hate you.'

Tessa stares at her. *Sex. What is it? Forbidden. Mary Magdalene was a prostitute. Surely Jenny must be much less than that. What has Jenny done that is so wrong? She just loves him.*

Tessa bends towards Jenny. She stoops a little so that her black hair intermingles with Jenny's blondeness. She encircles her with her arms. 'I love you Jenny. Always.' They hold each other.

***

Tessa's tired when she gets home. As usual, her mother's waiting for her. Mrs Kassis wants to talk about washing the windows which haven't been done for months, and she needs help carrying in the fruit she bought at the market, and she desperately needs Tessa's advice on what to cook for Sunday lunch when the cousins visit.

Shut up you boring woman. Just shut up. She looks at her mother with barely controlled disgust and then sees. Her mother is tired, small. She urgently moves boxes and fruit and plates, creating the order Mr Kassis expects. Tessa wants to knock her down for her stupidity, her wasted days, and to pick her up and hold her because she's the mother who always loves her.

She helps her mother with the chores and the decisions. At dinner she eats silently. Finally, she's allowed to go to her room. She sits at her desk, looking out over the park across the road. Her icon is near her lamp and she puts it in the drawer. She doesn't want to think about her church. *What would I do if it were me, not Jenny? To be pregnant now, when you're only a student, and not married.*

Tessa shivers. *My father would throw me out. He couldn't stand the shame. And my mother would cry. There'd be nowhere to go. I'd be so scared. There'd only be the refuge with all those crying children and frightened women.*

Tessa scratches incomplete lines and words in her notebook. She doesn't know how she can help Jenny. She writes to Athena. It seems so long since they've seen each other. It's autumn now. She can see the leaves on the huge liquidambars becoming golden. It's not cold yet, but she's cold. She gets up and turns on the heater. The warmth makes her feel Athena is there. I have to be there for Jenny.

Chapter 10

The next day is exhausting with lectures, study, Professor Davids' tutorial. She's irritated by his energy because it makes no room for other people's moods and feelings. Tessa doesn't stop to talk to him when the tutorial ends and she sees him watch her rushing out of the hall. She hurries towards the quadrangle lawn. Jenny's sitting with her head bowed looking at a piece of paper in her hands. She's pretty in a pale-yellow dress with her blonde hair tied into two plaits. She hands Tessa the paper. It's the address of a clinic.

'You don't have to come with me.'

'What is it?'

Jenny whispers. 'I can't have it.'

'Do you mean,' Tessa jerks out the words, 'not have the baby?'

Jenny nods.

'There are other things you can do?'

'What? Have a baby at nineteen when I can't cope with a baby? Stop university? I'll be all by myself. I'm scared. I just can't.' Jenny rubs her fingers, making them sore and red. 'Tony's studying. He's got no money and he hates this. He won't even talk about it and I just can't tell my parents.' Jenny looks up at Tessa. 'Please, I've been up all night, thinking and thinking. I can't think anymore.'

'It's illegal, Jenny.'

'There are ways around it, if you know where the good clinics are.' She pretends to smile, 'and if you have the money to pay for it.' Jenny rubs her eyes.' I've got savings from when I worked on the island.'

'Could you go to gaol?'

'I don't think so. Maybe. Can we stop talking about this? It's awful.'

Tessa hesitates. 'It's a sin, Jenny.'

'Yes, but it's my sin and I have to live with it. Look, it's all right, Tessa.' Jenny gets up and walks slowly along the footpath alone.

It's murder, Tessa keeps thinking. What would I do? I don't know. But can I judge? Maybe I should judge, but I'm ignorant. Jenny's nearly at the bus stop when Tessa starts running after her. 'Wait. Wait'

Tessa stands quietly at the bus stop with her friend. They board the bus quietly. They sit looking out of the bus window quietly. Tessa rests her hand over Jenny's. The bus trip takes half an hour. It stops not far from Tessa's home. They walk past beautiful Victorian houses with their carved brick detail and ironwork entrances. Enormous liquidambar trees with gnarled roots line the street. Jenny trips on the footpath which has been distorted by the huge roots, but she's safe because Tessa catches her. They murmur to each other. Tessa picks up big leaves from the ground, some of them brown, some of them yellowing. Jenny copies her. Suddenly Tessa throws them into the air and they watch them float like exotic dancers towards the footpath.

The clinic just looks like one of the houses. Jenny checks the number to make sure. They hold hands climbing the steps towards the front door. Jenny pushes against it. It's heavy, so they both push until it opens. A strong light sweeps through the front door and they turn their eyes downwards. It's white inside. A white lady approaches them and Jenny fills in a white form and they sit on white plastic chairs.

There are other girls, some with their mothers, some with boyfriends, some by themselves. One woman in her thirties sits blending into the white walls. She tells the sister that she just can't have anymore. A man in blue emerges occasionally from rooms behind other doors.

The white lady talks to Jenny and is kind. She lets Tessa go with her to a cubicle. Jenny twirls her plaits on top of her head, so that the white shapeless cap fits. She takes off her yellow dress and puts on a white cotton gown. Tessa ties the string at the back.

Jenny holds onto Tessa's hand so tightly, the orderly says. 'You have to let go.'

Jenny keeps shaking her head. 'I don't want to. I don't want to.'

'We can still leave, Jenny. Do you want to leave?'

Her grip loosens. 'No. I have to. I just... ' Her words slur into the anaesthetic as it starts working.

Tessa stays in the reception room waiting for the hours to pass. Jenny's fear, the doors closing, her loosening grip flit in and out of Tessa's thoughts. She jumps when the nurse calls her. 'She's in recovery. You can go and see her.'

There are metal railings around Jenny. She's white like the rest of the clinic now. The nurse is helping her. 'The anaesthetic has made her sick.'

She smells of vomit. Tessa sits by her bed. 'Are you all right Jenny?'

Jenny presses her stomach. 'I don't know,' she gasps. 'I feel empty.'

Tessa helps her out of the bed towards the cubicle. Jenny puts on her pale-yellow dress and releases the plaits from the hospital cap. They leave the clinic with instructions from the nurse to call immediately if there's too much bleeding. They walk down the steps, away from the heavy doors and the smells of anaesthetic. Jenny stops after a few steps, holding onto her stomach.

'Does it hurt?'

'Everything hurts.'

Tessa puts her arms around her. 'I know, Jenny.' And they cry on the beautiful tree-lined street.

Chapter 11

For a while Tessa clings to her home. She stops writing poetry, misses lectures, wants the safety of her family because she now knows that freedom is dangerous.

A letter arrives from Athena. She will never show her mother the letter because there are too many secrets.

Dearest Tessa

Jenny was really nice at school. Doesn't school feel like a million years ago?

I'm glad you didn't judge Jenny. It must be awful to be pregnant now. I think a lot more of you for supporting her, even though I know you think it is wrong. What she does has to be her decision not yours. You've just got to be there.

I've been promoted from coffee maker to junior, junior, junior... reporter. I miss you. Do you miss me now that you have new friends, your professor and writing?

It's wonderful about your distinctions. You used to say you couldn't do it. You can't say that now. I always knew the truth.

I'll write a longer letter soon and I'll be home by Christmas.

Love Athena

What happened in the Victorian house ties Jenny and Tessa together. They don't speak about it, but it's a forever bond between them. Tony tries to call Jenny a few times, but she refuses to see him. He just seems to disappear.

Tessa hadn't realised, that she'd changed. She can't remain locked in her home. She starts to chafe against the family's restrictions and begins to write again against her will. She has to go out, even if she's afraid of what's outside. She goes back to university lectures, but she's more cautious.

Professor Davids has been offered a two-year appointment in literature at Cambridge University and he'll be leaving before the year ends. He pressures his honours students and Tessa to work for him, even during the semester. He needs to finish his research before taking up the appointment.

Some of the students complain. Even though Tessa finds the additional workload difficult, she justifies it to Jenny. 'I'm learning so much,' she tells her as they wander down to The Pit.

Jenny shakes her head. 'Sure. He's got you worked out.'

Tessa ignores the comment.

An Elvis Presley song blares from The Pit. 'Hey, what's the noise?' Jenny calls out.

Joel hands her the morning's newspaper. 16 August 1977. Jenny hands it on to Tessa, then slumps into a chair.

There's chain smoking, black coffee, dope. Everyone's in mourning. What a waste of a life. Drug overdose. Tessa shudders at the memories of hypodermic needles lying under newspapers on her way to school, at the students casually smoking and taking speed, at pro-drug articles in the journal. The King is dead. Elvis Presley is dead.

Jenny holds her stomach. 'Elvis. Isn't it awful?' Tessa nods. 'Everything is awful.'

'Maybe.' Tessa rests her hand on Jenny's arm. 'It's not, you know.' Tessa waits for a moment. 'We have free will. There are choices.'

At home that night Mr Kassis disapproves of Elvis. 'I did not like that man or his music.' Tessa isn't allowed to turn on the radio that plays music in commemoration of Elvis Presley. 'Put on my songs, Tessa.' The bouzouki fills the lounge room strumming the folk songs Mr Kassis knew as a boy.

***

Tessa increasingly looks forward to the writing group. As she walks into The Pit a flying cup nearly hits her. 'Duck,' Carol calls out as it crashes against the wall. 'Sorry. It's only plastic and definitely meant for Joel.'

'It was only a joke.' When Joel laughs his green eyes make him look like a leprechaun.

'No more jokes about women.' Carol's fuming. 'It's the right time for the new sex discrimination laws. Joel needs them.'

'Are we still going on the picnic?' Tessa rustles her bag with bread, tomatoes and black olives.

'Sure. I've spent big money.' He grabs a paper bag and shows it off. 'Prawns!'

Carol huffs, but Tessa pipes in. 'Jenny's waiting for us.'

'Great. Come on, a joke's a joke. Let's go.'

Jenny waves half-heartedly when she sees them. Joel waves the bag of prawns. Carol shrugs. 'He'll never change.' Tessa sits on the rug. Jenny's quieter these days. She doesn't join in the talk about Elvis and writing and equal rights for women. Tessa glances at her. *How can there be equal rights when we're the ones who get pregnant?* Tony just walked away.

They eat bread and olives and watermelon that's been cut roughly so that it's jagged. 'Great food,' Joel says, spitting a black pip at Carol.

'You're revolting.' Carol whacks him on the arm, before pouring white wine into plastic cups.

They eat the prawns barbarically, with Joel decapitating them. Carol talks sympathetically to the prawns until even Jenny laughs. Joel jumps up and starts performing his latest poem about a watch dog. It's no ordinary woofer, but the heroic defender of non-sexist language. Attacked, nearly dead, doggy Joel struggles across the grass, barking feminist ideas until he lunges out and gives Carol a coughing fit.

'Enough,' Carol splutters. 'Okay, okay, you're a great comic satirist. I won't call you a male chauvinist pig, for a while anyway. My turn.' Carol's writing is always political. This time it's on selling uranium to the French and they argue over nuclear bombs and war. They finish their picnic discussing, imagining their possibilities and hopes. Joel disturbs the talk. 'Enough of all this philosophical soul searching. I've got a great idea.' Joel's animated again. 'Let's go to the reading at the University Hotel.' Tessa looks at him curiously. 'You know, there's a group of writers who read and perform their work there once a month. Next one is on Tuesday. We can have a drink first and their hamburgers are great, then whoever wants to can read their writing.' He doesn't wait for answers. 'So it's organised. I'll see you all there.'

Joel and Carol go off to classes. Tessa packs her basket while Jenny folds the rug. 'It'll be difficult for me to go to the reading.'

Jenny looks up. 'The reading?' She looks distracted as she puts the rug under her arm.

'Are you all right?'

Jenny shakes. her head. 'No, I want to cry a lot.' She presses her lips together. 'It's hard since the clinic.' She whispers. 'I wish it didn't happen.'

'I know, Jenny.'

***

Tessa opens the front door to face her mother's bustle. Mrs Kassis is clearing the cupboards. 'This is for the fete.' She piles tea towels on the table. 'We have never used them. I need your help Tessa.'

'What fete?'

Her mother looks surprised. 'You heard the priest at the church.' Tessa shakes her head. 'He is raising money for a new school. A Greek school. There will be a fete.'

She shudders. A school with even less freedom than she had as a school girl. 'No, I didn't hear.' Tessa walks away from her mother. 'I've got an assignment to do now. I'll help on the weekend.' *I don't want to think about a stupid fete.* Her mother starts to protest but Tessa is gone. She walks quickly up the stairs away from her mother, away from the sitting room with her father and tradition.

Tessa commences a series of lies that she introduces between breakfast and gardening, between Sunday church and bedtime. 'I have a compulsory lecture on Tuesday night. Everyone has to go. I'm giving a paper.' Mr Kassis becomes familiar with the idea, so that when

Tessa finally raises the University Hotel, he has already considered it. 'Well, then. You may go with your brother.'

Yes. Yes. She races to Peter's room to tell him half the truth. 'We're going to the University Hotel on Tuesday night.' She'll explain that it's her writing group later. Much later. Tessa is amazed at her ability to manipulate and her sense of control, but she's careful. Independence is brittle. Independence. *Do I want it? I don't want to end up like Jenny. Is that independence?*

***

Tessa goes most days to help Professor Davids who's struggling to finish his work before Cambridge. He doesn't hear her when she enters his rooms. She has to say hello three times until she laughs. 'You're like my father, single-minded.'

'What?' He looks up. 'Are you insulting me, Tessa?'

'I'm not sure if I am or not. At least my father wouldn't get into such a mess.' She moves between his papers and books.

'Single-minded, am I? Well, I've had enough of this.' He stands up. 'Let's get out of here.' Occasionally between lectures and research they share conversation, wandering around the university grounds with its old trees and buildings.

Tessa rattles on about her mother's vegetable garden. 'She grew up with fresh food. It's like a tradition. You know traditions are important to my family.'

'And to mine, Tessa.' He directs her along another pathway. 'I like the trees down here.' He strokes his moustache. 'Tradition. I used to go with my father once a year to the synagogue for Yom Kippur, the Day of Atonement. Do you know what that is?'

She teases. 'No. Please do tell me, Professor Davids. '

'I will and don't be so cheeky. You'll be interested.' He teases back. 'It's the holiest day of the Jewish year. My father ate and drank nothing from sunset to sun fall the next day to atone for his sins.'

'I know all about fasting and atonement, unfortunately,' Tessa quips.

'It was his act of repentance, even though he didn't need to repent. I suspect I should have done the atonement instead of him.' David stops beside a tall thin tree with branches that twist into eerie shapes. 'I miss going to the synagogue with him.'

He runs his hand along the rough, peeling bark of the tree, and Tessa quivers. It's as though he's running his hands against her. Tessa looks at him curiously. *You're not Heathcliff. You're not.*

He motions to Tessa to smell the grey-green leaves crushed in his cupped palms. Bending, she smells the eucalyptus intermingling with his maleness. 'Lovely, isn't it? What's it remind you of?'

You. She looks at him surprised, then answers. 'The bush... rivers.' They wander further along the path, giving her time to dissipate unclear desires. 'Are you religious, David?'

He think s carefully before he answers. 'I believe in God. Is that religious?'

Tessa nods. 'Are you Jewish?'

'I don't know. Probably not.' He thinks awhile. 'I suppose when my father married my mother and brought up boys who didn't have bar mitzvahs, when they became men at thirteen, he wasn't part of the community anymore. It was sad for him. My father missed the Jewish life.'

'My father wouldn't know how to live, if he didn't have his Greek Church and his Greek life.'

They end their walk and Tessa pretends to herself that their talks will always be there.

'Tessa, I'll see you tomorrow then for serious work. No garden walks for a while.'

'Yes, tomorrow.' He doesn't look at her. He's back at his desk engrossed in plans and preparations for his future. Tessa turns away confused.

She arrives home to a mother who's also engrossed. Even though the fete is months away, the preparations fill Mrs Kassis with an energy that makes it a daily preoccupation. Bending, Tessa helps her mother pack hand-knitted baby booties in cellophane, but it's eucalyptus and bark that weave strange patterns in her mind. Mr Kassis watches, tired from his day at the factory. Opening the Hellenic paper, he enjoys reading its mixture of Australian and Greek news until he notices a report. He reads aloud, '17 September 1977. Maria Callas, the famous Greek opera singer, has died of a heart attack at fifty-three, abandoned by her Greek lover, Aristotle Onassis.'

'You see, Tessa what happens to even great people. Maria Callas sang like the earth and the wind and the storm. A gift from God, but she spat upon God and she sinned and died alone, Tessa. She was punished alone, Tessa.' Mrs Kassis nods agreement as she puts olive green ribbons around the cellophane.

Tessa does not say anything. Her throat feels like sand.

'Has there been post?' Mr Kassis looks at his wife.

'Sorry, but I forgot to look in the letterbox with the fete and... '

Before her mother finishes, Tessa gets up to go to the mailbox, glad to leave the cellophane and baby booties and the lounge room with its ornaments and floral lounge.

Tessa inhales deeply, coughing the roughness out of her throat, smelling the scents of the garden. There are business letters for her father. She's curious at the thick envelope caught at the bottom. Her heart jumps. It's from Athena. Tearing open the envelope, Tessa reads.

Dearest Tessa

Love. I'm in love. It's wonderful, romantic, disastrous. Christos. He's a wild Greek reporter on the paper. He towers over me and has the most beautiful blue eyes and curly lack hair. He's twenty-six and drinks too much, laughs too much, risks too much. He'll shock you. He shocks me.

I've moved out of my cousin's house and there's scandal. My relatives are furious. I'm just waiting until they tell my parents and then it'll be hell. What do you think of me, I wonder? Don't judge me, please.

We've exchanged vows to each other on the Acropolis, surrounded by ancient marble columns and the temple honouring the Goddess Athena. Christos insists that the temple is dedicated to me, because he worships me. That's not true of course, but I want to believe him. He says he needs me and I love him. Love is so sweet. Do you remember? I'm sending you my little piece of the Acropolis.

Please keep it and be happy for me.

One day, I hope we can walk together on the white sands of our Greek Islands like I promised you. For now, I'll run along the sands with Christos.

Love Athena

Tessa touches the smooth marble, with its jagged crystal edges that glisten in the last light of the day. She puts it against her cheek and it's cool.

Athena, I don't want to judge.

Chapter 12

Tessa is careful to please her parents all weekend and on Monday and Tuesday. She's compliant and runs to make her father's coffee. She's compliant and listens to her mother talk about the fete. Tuesday night arrives at last. Peter is allowed to drive Mr Kassis' car. There are Papa's warnings. 'Drive slowly.' 'Call us when you arrive.' 'Be home early.'

When the car door slams shut, Tessa starts giggling. 'What's so funny?' Tessa can't stop. She giggles and splutters until they're nearly there and Peter is going to kill her.

'Sorry, sorry.' Tessa calms down. 'I don't know. It's just the escape.'

'You're strange sometimes, Tessa.'

The University Hotel is busy. Green doors lead into a noisy public bar, with men and women drinking. Peter raises his eyebrows. 'Tessa, are you sure we're in the right place?' He looks older than seventeen with his stocky build and dark complexion, and he hopes no one asks for his ID. He's been into pubs before, without his parents' knowledge.

A television blares from one corner and the sign 'Bistro' flashes over a bar. 'It's this way.' Tessa moves to avoid a collision with a man who's drunk a bit too much, and heads to the bistro. Peter follows. There are people sitting at tables eating and drinking. Then she sees a hand waving . A voice calls across the room. 'Over here. Here.'

Introducing her brother, Tessa is uncomfortable as Peter's conservatism grates against Joel's excited

105

liberalism. Tessa feels restricted by her brother and sits quietly, while Joel pours cheap Riesling into glasses and Carol passes the nachos around. Cheese slides off the corn chips, splattering on Peter's shirt. He's annoyed.

Joel jumps up. 'Let's get good seats.' He leads them into a room set aside for performances. It's a mixed audience, mostly young. A man in his twenties with earrings and an Aboriginal flag on his T-shirt sits next to a lesbian couple kissing. Girls in crop-tops with psychedelic pants and guys with long hair and head bands hang over chairs. Peter grabs Tessa's arm. 'What's this about?'

'It's just creative writing. You were the one who said I should keep writing.'

'Sure.' He's sarcastic. 'You've been lying and now you've got me right in the middle of it. What am I going to tell the parents?'

'Nothing. You have to promise. Nothing. Just let me read my poetry and we'll go. Okay? Okay?' She begs and bribes. 'Look, I'll do your next English essay.'

He shakes his head. 'English essay? I don 't know. It's not the point, is it?'

'Please, Peter.'

He's scowling, as he sits beside Tessa. Carol reads her story. She ends with her hand in the air, calling out. 'Feminist Mary Daly's right. Courage to be, is the key to revelatory power of the feminist revolution.' The lesbian couple stop to clap. Joel whistles and Carol thanks the whistler. Tessa avoids Peter's eyes. She's glad that Jenny's sitting on the other side of her.

Joel runs to centre stage. Stretching out his arms he draws the audience towards him, laughing as he makes his tall, boyish physique twist and turns. Tessa avoids looking at Peter as the crowd laughs at his performance of a fractured fairy tale where he strips for 'The Emperor's New Clothes'. He leaves on his underpants, even though the crowd is screaming – Take them off. Take them off.' Peter crosses his arms.

Tessa waits until the audience is quieter. She edges slowly towards the reading space, then stands still. Her plain black jumper and plain black skirt are austere in the room filled with individuality and colour. She begins.

a young girl
dedicates two months
to ritual stripping of flesh
in rites of atonement.
In the third month, she'll leave
her core exposed
nowhere to conceal
inadequacies
 parental desires
men defiling a Jewish grave
fairy penguins flapping oil slicks...

Peter refuses to talk to Tessa on the way home. The parents are waiting up for them. Tessa has to answer their questions, before she's given permission to go to her room. She doesn't tell them about the lesbian couple or that she read to strangers in a hotel or that she lied to them and her brother. Her mother kisses her goodnight. 'I am glad you enjoyed yourself, Tessa.'

As she walks upstairs with her brother she whispers.

'I'm sorry Peter. It wasn't fair to you.'

'That's right. It wasn't.'

'Will you tell them?'

'No. Not this time.' He slams the door of his bedroom shut.

The next day Tessa meets Jenny at The Pit. Everyone's working on the second edition of the journal. Joel comes over to them and talks about the readings until Tessa turns her back on him. 'Yes, a great night.' *I'm a liar. Liar. Liar.*

Tessa helps Jenny cut and paste. Jenny puts down the paste and wipes her hands on a cloth. 'I'd like you to come with me somewhere.' Tessa looks at her curiously. 'I've been thinking about it for a while. It's just that we have to have some control, not just let things happen to us. That's right, isn't it? '

'What are you talking about?'

'I couldn't stand ever going through it again,' she says under her breath. 'The clinic. I've made an appointment for this afternoon at the uni Family Planning rooms. Could you come with me? I need you.' Tessa doesn't answer. 'Please, Tessa.'

'I don't want to.'

'I'm scared, Tessa.'

She looks at Jenny. 'All right, I'll come.'

The Family Planning Clinic is in one of the terraces Tessa passes on her way to university. Her stomach knots, as she follows Jenny up the narrow steps. There's a waiting room. The receptionist takes their names. A toy box sits casually in the corner. Pamphlets on birth control are piled on a table. An explicit poster on sexually transmitted diseases is stuck on the wall.

The receptionist calls their names. They stand up and follow her into a room, where a doctor is sitting behind a desk. She doesn't wear a white coat and gets up when they enter. 'Please sit down, Make yourselves comfortable.' They sit uncomfortably on grey vinyl chairs. 'How can I help you?'

Jenny looks at Tessa, then at the doctor. She takes a breath. 'We want to know about contraception.' Tessa bites her nails. The doctor doesn't ask the reasons. She takes out a variety of packets and brochures and talks about condoms and the pill and IUDs and abstinence.

The doctor is matter-of-fact. 'If you have sexual partners, the best contraception is a condom. It protects you from possible infection and ensures, in 97 per cent of cases that you won't get pregnant.'

'Tessa interrupts. This isn't for me. I'm just here as a friend.'

The doctor smiles. 'You're a good friend then. But it doesn't hurt to know about contraception, does it?' She continues. 'If you plan to have a permanent relationship, then it would probably be best to use a low estrogen pill.' The doctor explains each contraceptive option. 'Have you any questions?' Jenny asks a bit more about the IUDs. 'Do you want to ask anything?' she looks at Tessa. She shakes her head. 'Well, I'll give you these sample condoms and write out prescriptions for the pill, just in case. You'll be free to choose what you want to do.'

'I don't need it.' Tessa reddens. *I hate freedom. I hate this.*

The doctor walks with them to the door. 'Come and visit if you have a question, a problem or just want to talk anytime.'

They walk away from the sandstone terrace, across the park to the university. 'We learnt something, didn't we Tessa?'

'That was... I don't know.' Tessa bites a nail.

'Thanks for coming with me.'

'Look I bought something for you.' Jenny takes out a box from her bag. 'Since we're both nineteen and mature, thinking adults...' Tessa opens the box, then starts laughing.

'So, you like it, then?'

'Yes.' Tessa reads the inscription on the coffee mug. 'You Are Woman.'

Jenny becomes serious. 'Was it okay, about seeing the doctor and everything?'

Tessa holds her mug in both hands. 'Yes, Jenny, it was okay.'

'Can I do something for you?'

Tessa nods. 'It's a little old shop not far from here. Can we go there?'

They walk quietly along the footpath through the streets bordering the university. Old ladies emerge from small houses and mothers push strollers. Pensioners wait in the red striped barber shop and students get haircuts in unisex hair salons. Health food stores and cheap cafes are dotted between dress boutiques. 'Over there.' Tessa points to a crammed shop, with a stuffed zebra outside its door.

They peer into its dingy, dark window. Toasters and radios and the flotsam of people's lives sit beside each other. Tessa and Jenny push past the goods piled beside the door. They look through the glass of a locked display cabinet. Old jewellery and ornaments lie on purple velvet beds. Tessa points to a square silver case. She asks the small lady behind the counter to unlock the display cabinet and let them look at it. There are intricate engravings depicting flowers and birds in flight. 'It's beautiful.' Tessa hands it to Jenny. 'Peter can use this for cards.' She pauses. 'Or for nothing at all. Do you think he'll like it? It's for his school graduation.'

'Yes. He will, Tessa.'

'It'll remind him of art and music and something else besides law.'

The small lady wraps the silver box in brown paper.

Chapter 13

Tessa and Mrs Kassis fold the washing together. 'I got a high distinction for my last essay.'

Mrs Kassis smiles at her daughter. 'You are a clever girl, Tessa.' Mrs Kassis sings old Greek melodies as she works. Tessa doesn't tell her that her poems are going to be published in a literary journal under the name Tessa. She doesn't tell her that she refuses a surname that would link her to her father and mother. Joel wants to celebrate Tessa's success and after their writing meeting he flourishes a twenty-dollar note. 'Coming Carol and Jenny? We have to toast our famous writer.' Joel puts his arms around Tessa's waist, lifting her as he makes a sweeping turn. 'You're a lunatic, Joel.' Tessa blushes.

Jenny has a new waitressing job. 'Got to work. Sorry everyone. It's great news, Tessa.' Carol, Joel and Tessa go to the local pub, which is even nosier than the University Hotel. Joel pushes past some men drinking, holding Tessa's hand so that she's dragged behind him. He finds a table and orders drinks without asking anyone what they want.

Carol shakes her head. 'You'll never change. You're such a male chauvinist pig.'

'Oink, oink.' Joel laughs. 'Now say thank you for the drinks.'

Carol hits him half-jokingly. Joel claims that he's been wounded for life and his arm needs a sling. Tessa, you'll have to stroke my shoulder to take away the pain.' Tessa shakes her head, laughing, and he takes her hands, kissing them. 'Chips everyone?' Joel disappears into the crowd.

Carol sips her glass of wine. 'Do you like Joel?'

'Yes, don't you? '

Carol pauses. 'You haven't been around. Look, I just want to tell you,' she finishes her wine, Joel likes you a lot. He's going to play around with you. If that's what you want too it's not an issue.'

Tessa starts to object when Joel appears with packets of every kind of chip. 'Couldn't decide which one you liked, so I bought them all.'

'You're so generous,' Carol mocks.

The afternoon passes happily with drinking and talking and jokes. They toast Tessa's soon-to-be-published work before Carol leaves to meet some other friends. Tessa and Joel walk back towards the university, but they stop halfway and sit under a huge Moreton Bay fig in the parklands. Tessa runs her hand along its knotty root. 'It's amazing to think this tree has probably been more than two hundred years.'

'Looks good for its age,' Joel grins. They sit cross-legged looking out over the park. Joel pulls his light brown hair back into a pony tail, then lets it loose across his face again. 'You know Tessa, I really want to be an actor, except I get scared that I won't make it. It's pretty tough out there.'

'You'll make it. You're talented. At the reading everyone was eating out of your hand. You'll be a star, Joel.' It's pleasant in the spring sun and they lie on their backs talking. Then they are silent, resting on the new grass.

Tessa doesn't know how it happens. Maybe it's the soft breeze and the afternoon wine. It feels natural as Joel fingers the buttons on her blouse. She watches his hands with detachment, observing the ease with which he teases the pearl buttons out of the cotton slots, leaving them open. He runs his hands down her throat, pushing the slots apart, reaching under her plain white bra. She closes her eyes as his hands explore the heaviness of her breasts and the rippling of her nipples, and she feels his mouth against her neck. Images of another time filter into Tessa's thoughts as she leans towards him. 'Athena.' Suddenly she opens her eyes. She sits up, startling Joel. Then she starts pushing him away, forcing her pearl buttons back into their slots.

He fights against her hands. 'Don't, Joel. Don't.' He won't stop and she shouts, making passers-by turn so that he has to stop. She jumps up, brushing grass and leaves from her skirt.

'What's wrong Tessa?'

'This is wrong.'

'It's not.'

'For me, it is.' She turns away from him. 'You know, if we do this we won't be friends anymore.'

He grabs her hand. 'That's not true.'

'Let me go, Joel. This is stupid.' She pulls her hand away. 'Look, I'll see you at the next writing meeting. All right?'

'No, it's not all right.' Joel stares at her. Tessa stares back. 'All right, I'll go.' He turns away sharply, walking away, then jogging, running. His movements are youthful, with a barely controlled energy. Tessa watches him. She bites her lip. It would have only been an interlude for him, a disaster for her. *I don't love you, Joel. At least Jenny was in love.*

That evening after dinner she helps her mother with her preparations for the fete. She wonders if her father suspects her other life. Mr Kassis watches her carefully as she moves jams and boxes into the back seat of their station wagon, for the fete the next day. She doesn't dare look at him. Her mother is invigorated by the control of ordering the cakes and biscuits in piles, labelling jars and tins. The priest actually gave her a special mention at last Sunday's service. Finally, the car is stacked and Tessa excuses herself with a kiss, leaving her mother flushed with last minute touches.

Tessa wakes the next morning to Mrs Kassis' hand stroking her cheek. 'We must be early.' She leaves to knock on Peter's door. Breakfast is rushed. Mrs Kassis urgent. The fete.

They are one of the first families there. Peter helps erect the stalls with Mr Kassis. Tessa has been volunteered to work on the white elephant stall with Mrs Pappas. Mrs Kassis is arranging the cake stall.

Tessa enjoys sorting the bits and pieces discarded by their owners. She picks up a porcelain duck with some of its blue paint rubbed off and puts it away for Athena. *Athena. Only two months and she's back.* The duck had looked sad among the smart plastic toys and modern containers. She'll put the blue porcelain duck on her shelf at home until Athena can claim it.

People look around the stall. Some buy, some bargain, some complain there's nothing there for them. Mrs Pappas fiddles and repacks. The sun comes through the clouds and Mrs Pappas complains about the heat.

Tessa watches the way her mouth moves, the pencilled lines on her forehead intensifying as she complains. Tessa nods agreement and from time to time looks interested. She notices Mrs Pappas's faded prettiness and wonders if her hopes are unfulfilled, like her mother's, like the other women of that generation.

Mrs Pappas's son walks with Mrs Kassis to the white elephant stall. Mrs Kassis addresses her daughter. 'There are enough women on the cake stall now. I have to come to work on the elephant stall and give you time to enjoy the fete, Tessa.'

'You're the best mother.' Mrs Kassis smiles at her daughter.

John Pappas walks silently with Tessa between the ponies and the puppet shows and fairy floss, until she escapes onto the Ferris wheel with one of her cousins. John Pappas is waiting for her when she finishes the ride. He follows her dutifully as she giggles with her cousin on the camel ride, then is painted as a tiger at the face paint stand, and finally explores the garden stall. People start to pack up, forcing Tessa and her cousin to stop racing from stall to stall. John Pappas buys them orange juices before escorting them back to their parents.   '

The fete finishes and the few things not sold are packed to send to the Salvation Army. Women gather to discuss the success of the fete, while the men dismantle the stands. Mr Kassis gives Tessa the giant panda bear he won for her on the lucky wheel and she playfully kisses him. Mrs Kassis is glowing with the generous praise everyone's given her for her jams. They liked the kumquat jam best,' she says, making Tessa giggle. Peter shows his mother an old coat stand that he plans to sand and varnish. Everyone enters the car happy.

'It was a good day,' Mr Kassis approves.

When they arrive home, there is a package left at the door with a note from the neighbour. 'This was put in the wrong mail box.'

Mrs Kassis bends to pick it up, but she is too slow. Tessa grabs it. 'It's from Athena.' Holding it tightly, she kisses her mother quickly and races to her room while her mother calls to her.

'Remember dinner is soon. I need your help.'

'Yes. Yes. Yes.'

Dear Tessa

Christos is truly the opposite of his name, an anti-christ. That's a dramatic thing to write, but I want to be dramatic. I feel like a Greek tragedy where the heroine is betrayed. He told me that he'd finished sowing his wild oats as he was brushing back his black hair. He has such beautiful hair. He's so handsome. He said he wanted to plant a field of flowers with me.

Christos took me to wild tavernas where we drank too much and he smashed plates and aroused my deepest sensuality, but he's not mine. He's hurt me. He said the other women meant nothing to him, that I held his heart. It's a lie.

Is that what men are like? I remember when I was ten, hiding behind a door listening to my parents fight after my mother had discovered my father had a mistress. My father never told her the truth, but she knew he'd had other mistresses. I saw him once, arm in arm with a strange woman. My mother changed after that fight. She didn't care about him so much anymore and she took up art courses. I don't want that. I just don't. I know my mother's sad inside and I know that's all Christos can give me.

Anyway, enough of Christos, there's a package with this letter. The hand-carved donkeys carrying wood are just like the donkeys of the villages here. I bought them on your birthday, for your birthday. It's late. Look into the eyes of the donkeys. They're soft eyes, even though they're carved in wood and their owners carry such heavy loads.

I will be coming home early - in a month.

Love you always.

Athena

Tessa reads and re-reads Athena's letter. Love Is dangerous. Freedom is dangerous. Tessa puts the wooden donkeys with the soft eyes beside her Starry Moon shell. She puts her hands over her eyes and smiles. Athena will be home soon.

Chapter 14

At the next creative writing workshop Tessa is distant towards Joel. She sits between Carol and Jenny. 'The D.H. Lawrence elective is going ahead next year,' she announces.

'Fantastic.' Jenny smiles.

'Are you going to write about it for the next journal?' Carol asks.

'Imagine that. We can change decisions. I will write an article.'

Joel moves over to Tessa and whispers in her ear. 'Sorry about the other day. Things got out of hand. Is it okay now?'

Tessa looks directly into his eyes. 'Yes.' *But it isn't, you know Joel. You were wrong and so was I.*

Jenny leaves for lectures. She's more serious about her studies lately. Tessa goes to help Professor Davids, whose work is piled on his desk. His voice comes from behind the pile. 'When will this all be finished?' Tessa burrows into the pile, sorting essential from non-essential papers. 'I appreciate your help Tessa. And the others' too.'

'Well, you have worked us all nearly to death'

A laugh emerges from the papers. 'To death? Tessa, aren't you exaggerating a little? This has been good experience for you all.'

She smiles. 'I don't know about that.' Quietly she adds, 'It'll be different when you leave.'

'You'll have time to go out with your friends.' A chill runs down her spine. She knows that without the professor's research there'll be fewer excuses to escape from her family and the community. There's the ball soon, as well. The Greek Young Matrons' Association's annual ball raises money for the children's hospital. The Kassis family will be sitting at one of the main tables because Mr Kassis donates so much. Tessa flinches, remembering last year's white meringue dresses clumsily waltzing around the floor with their black liquorice partners in bow ties. This year her mother wants her to wear a white meringue dress. *I won't. I won't.*

'Athena is coming back. I can't wait to see her.' She glances up at Professor Davids. She doesn't tell him that she'll miss going in and out of his rooms, miss the familiarity between them, miss him.

He suddenly pushes the books on his desk aside. 'Enough work. Let's go for a walk.'

'I have to finish this.' He takes her hand, pulling her away from the desk. 'All right, all right, I'm coming. Where are we going?'

'Wherever you like. I need to get out of this stuffy room and away from students knocking on my door.'

'The flowers behind the tennis courts should be budding. Can we look at them?' She's been working in her father's garden in the last few weeks making sure the spring insects don't burrow into the unbudded pods, destroying them before they've had a chance to bloom.

As they stroll towards the gardens, Professor Davids talks about Cambridge and the opportunity to research from original documents. 'You'll be doing that one day, Tessa.'

'I don't think so.'

'I do. But for now, you should enrol in honours for next year.'

'I'd like that.'

Workmen are hammering in trellises for hyacinth to climb. They wander past them to the roses. Tessa stops to smell the scent of a white rose. Her black hair intermingles with the petals and thorns. It catches and Professor Davids disentangles the strands. 'Be careful.'

'I'm always careful. That's me.' They wander between the red prickly banksia and traditional English-carnations. Tessa starts laughing. 'This garden has a serious identity problem. It's not sure if it's wild Australian bush or a rustic British green patch.'

'Maybe it's both. My plants don't have to worry. They're happy if they just survive. Maybe I should give them to you while I'm away.'

'Well, you'll have to let me see them.'

'Yes, maybe another time.'

'There isn't another time. Let me see your poor plants. I could save them.'

'I don't know.' He doesn't want to take Tessa to his university residence, but she's soft and teasing and they're both tired from the months of work. She's insistent. 'Okay, just for a few minutes. For plant classification and lifesaving.'

David unlocks his door. His room has an unmade double bed on one side and scattered books and unwashed cups on a coffee table. 'I was working late last night. It's not an excuse, just an explanation.'

Tessa smiles. 'It looks like your rooms.'

'Come and see my pathetic garden.' He opens the balcony door, sliding it to one side. Tessa follows. She digs her hands into the soil in the planter box, turning it, feeling the blackness.

'It's dry and hard. You're starving your plants. Stay here.' She finds the kitchen and brings back water and pours it into the box. 'Bougainvillea. It's lovely, except you've got to watch out for the long thorns - worse than roses, but the colour is pinker, redder than roses.'

'Your hands are dirty, Tessa.' He takes out his handkerchief and stares at her hands. 'Soft,' he murmurs and instinctively kisses the tips so that his moustache brushes against them. She giggles nervously. He takes her hands, drawing her inside the room.

David touches her lips, lightly, gently at first, like a woman, and she remembers schoolgirl reflections on a lake. His mouth presses against hers but it's different, more urgent. Passively she lets him kiss and taste her lips, tongue, mouth, but it's she who's savouring his warmth and she wants to stay in his arms because it feels safe, unconfusing.

They lie on his unmade bed with his hands rolling her nipples like she'd done herself, like Athena had done, like Joel. She pushes Joel out of her thoughts. David's moustache rubbing her skin, his tongue wetting, his mouth sucking make her feel like a child and a woman. She bends her head against his arm, crying into him so that he can't hear or see the crying. He rubs her skin until it goose-bumps into needs and urges and she holds onto him. His hands explore the black curling hair that only she knows about in the mirror of her bedroom and he presses his hands into her until she feels he should never stop.

Suddenly, it's as if her father's watching. She's afraid and starts pushing, shoving the hands away, moving away, whispering 'No, no. Please don't. Please.' Pleading David away, pleading. He doesn't stop and she wants him to go on, but she forces his hands away until he's not touching her, until he's only heavy breathing.

Tessa can't look at him. He rolls away. His breathing is less laboured, shallow, as they lie beside each other, but separate. Tessa whispers, 'You hate me.'

He doesn't answer. Turns towards her. He puts his arms around her, pressing his head against her, stroking her face gently. 'No, Tessa. Never.'

***

It's the weekend. Tessa avoids her father's eyes. She drops a plate as she clears the breakfast table. It shatters on the floor and her father shouts at her as he leaves for work. 'What is wrong with you?' He works on Saturdays and is in a hurry. He doesn't wait for an answer.

Mrs Kassis talks and talks about the fete and the money to be raised for the new Greek school until Tessa runs out of the room. That Sunday she chants the psalms in her church. She smiles at the people who say hello. She accepts the priest's blessing and feels like a hypocrite. There's relief when Sunday ends and she can be alone.

David's leaving for Cambridge in ten days. She doesn't tell Jenny about what happened. Anyway, Jenny is too distracted by her new love James, to think about anyone else. 'I think he's really nice, except I'm nervous.' She goes off to meet James for coffee and

Tessa goes to David's rooms. David is distant as he talks about his trip.

Tessa bends her head. Maybe he doesn't want her. She murmurs 'Don't worry about the other day.'

He leaves his work and stands up. 'Tessa, I am worried. You're my student.'

I'm an adult, not a schoolgirl. Anyway, you're leaving, so you're not even my lecturer.'

He starts to pace the room. 'What happened compromises my position and yours.' He stops moving. Tessa, it's more than that. You're from somewhere else. I shouldn't be involved or get you involved. I'd have an affair with you and that's not good enough.'

'I can make decisions for myself. It's my responsibility, not yours.'

He's only half-listening to her. 'I don't want to marry anyone and that's the only right thing to do.'

'I don't want to be married.'

He shakes his head. 'Maybe not today, but you'll get married and you'll be a virgin, like you've been taught.'

She whispers. 'I don't care.'

'I do care.' Tessa looks away from him, trying to stop tears.

'Don't you think I want you?' He puts his arms around her. 'Of course, I want you. You're beautiful and questioning and gentle.' He strokes her hair. 'My parents never reconciled their religions and traditions. My father wanted his Jewishness and my mother didn't understand. I'm not part of your culture and I'll make you unhappy in the end, whatever happens.'

Tessa leans against him. 'I don't understand anything you're saying. I trust you.'

I don't want to be trusted, Tessa.'

***

They see each other every day. Sometimes they work together, sometimes they talk through the university grounds, but always they go to his apartment where Tessa turns the soil of his plants and seeks his books and him.

He's gentle as he explores her body and she loves the sensuality. She discovers that her heavy breasts and downy arms are sexual. That his hands touching her fulfil a yearning. She slowly traces his chest with her lips, giggling as the hairs tickle her nose, stroking his moustache, kissing his face until he's laughing and there's pleasure and gentleness. She doesn't care about her father or mother or the icon hidden in her desk drawer.

He's naked and she puts her hands over her eyes, making David smile. 'Tessa, you're young.' Gently he takes her hands away from her face. 'Put your arms around me.'

It's a relief to hold onto him so that she doesn't have to think as he presses against her, as they move rhythmically together until she's gasping, holding him tighter, until he's calling out.

David's careful to leave her a virgin, but she's initiated, nestling under his arm in his bed. He strokes her body. Afterwards they're quiet, listening to David 's classical tapes. Tessa imagines that he won't leave, that the afternoon will go on and on. She whispers, 'You're going away for so long.'

'I'll be coming back.' He touches her cheek. She rests her head against him.

She traces his moustache with her fingers. 'I'll miss you. Will you write to me?'

'Yes.'

She catches her breath. 'I love you.'

He kisses her tenderly. Then he's gone.

At home, Tessa stays in her room. She opens her dresser drawer looking for Athena's letters. They are alongside her combs and brushes. Taking out her brush, she strokes her hair in long heavy movements, then puts down her brush. She finds a tape and puts it into the recorder. There's nothing to say at first as she listens to the tape whirring forward. She stops it, rewinds.

'Athena, I promised to send you a tape. I'm sending this by sea. It will take a while to reach you, but it will have been a romantic journey, an adventure.

'You know I fell in love with my Professor Davids. I call him David. You would have liked him. He made me think and took me on a perilous journey. A journey into my feelings. I know what sexuality is now. Don't worry though, my father is safe. I'm still *'pure'*. I want to laugh when I say that. Pure. I understand Jenny now. I'm glad I didn't blame her. I don't know enough about anything to judge anyone. David has left for Cambridge and there's no one to put their arms around me and make me feel special and he's gone and I love him.

'I understand about Christos too.' Tessa cries and the tape records it.

Chapter 15

She studies harder than she's ever done before. She pretends to be interested in the Greek Young Matrons' Ball until her mother talks about the nice young men there. 'You have been asked about,' Tessa.' She escapes into the garden, digging and turning the soil until her mother calls her again. 'Come inside, Tessa. It is enough.'

Tessa writes in her room and meets the writing group once a week. They criticise her poetry. 'It's like you're not telling the truth anymore,' Carol says. 'It's glib.' Jenny defends her, but Tessa knows her writing is a lie. She cringes. *Maybe I can't write anymore. She puts down her pen. I don't care. I miss David so much.* She has lunch with Jenny, who keeps asking what's wrong until Tessa is trapped into telling her about David. 'I'm sorry, Tessa.' Trying to make Tessa feel better, she talks less about James and about books until Tessa smiles.

Family duties, the Church, her parents have a sameness that stifles her. The writing group isn't enough. She's planted his bougainvillea alongside the back fence. Her father worries about the thorns, but appreciates the colour. There is no letter from David.

An urgent delivery from Athena arrives. Lying on her bed she carefully unsticks the flap, takes out the paper, pressing it flat against the starched linen.

Dearest Tessa

I have your tape and I want to hold you - but I'm too far away. Your professor is your first love. It's painful, I know. You risk being hurt when you love someone, because they can leave. But it was wonderful, wasn't it?

Would you rather not have known him? I'm sure he loves you.

What matters now is to go on with your literature. You said you're doing well in it. Be brilliant. Not because of your father or mother or David, but because of you.

I wish I could be there with you. I'm not. You think you're alone. You're not. You're strong.

You know I love you. Your words sent so slowly across the sea have upset me. I won't write about myself now. Another time.

Love Athena

Tessa holds Athena's letter as she moves towards her window and the familiar trees spreading leaves and colour into her room. The trees are beautiful. Riffling through her drawer she finds her icon. *Maybe I should pray. I haven't prayed for so long.*

Closing her eyes, she imagines David at Cambridge and Athena in Greece. So far away, but close too. She sits at her desk and writes.

Dear Athena

I hear you. I feel better, but still unsafe. I miss David, I miss you. You're right. I'll work even harder at my studies. I want to be brilliant.

I love you,

Tessa

***

It's Peter's last official day at school before exams. The auditorium is full for Speech Day. Tessa sits with her parents in the third row. Mr Kassis is wearing his navy-blue suit and well-pressed white shirt. Mrs Kassis wears her olive green paisley frock.

The summer day is humid, making the hall stifling as parents, teachers and students settle into the process of speeches and platitudes. Tessa shifts on her chair. Has it only been a year? I can't believe I did this only a year ago. Perspiration drips down her father's neck, and she watches him take out a large handkerchief to wipe his face.

The Headmaster commences the programme. 'There is Peter.' Mrs Kassis whispers excitedly. Peter is stocky like his father. He strides onto the stage to receive an honour prize. Peter looks out into the auditorium and flashes a smile at his parents and Tessa.

The grinding weeks of study and exams are about to start, but for now everyone is celebrating the end of school. The Kassis' have invited friends and relatives over for a party after the Speech Day.

They hurry back home to ensure everything is ready. Final touches are made before guests arrive, and the onslaught. Peter stands at the door with his father, to greet the arrivals and receive white envelopes with money inside. Tessa and Mrs Kassis wait on the women, who talk babies and gossip while the men argue politics and business. Children run among the adults, receiving an occasional slap from a parent. Then they continue their course of destruction. The priest makes a token visit, honouring the family.

Tessa and Mrs Kassis serve quickly, smiling constantly, washing dishes only to return them to the table to be dirtied again. Tessa glimpses the interplay between her cousin's daughters and a new baby playing childish games, hugging and kissing, being women. John Pappas stands talking to Tessa's father.

He is tall, thickset, but handsome. Tessa notices women stare and admire.

Mr Kassis enjoys offering his relatives and friends hospitality on this occasion. He in his armchair watching is family move in and around the visitors. The guests leave unhurriedly, with the last child knocking over a vase of flowers with a startling crash. Peter and Mr Kassis move chairs and tables back into their traditional positions. Tessa and Mrs Kassis clean and put away dishes and leftover food, until Tessa says, 'Let's do it tomorrow. Aren't you tired? I am.'

Mrs Kassis looks cautiously at her husband. 'It was a wonderful party, but we are tired.'

He stops, turns to his wife and daughter. 'Go to bed then. This can wait. You have done well.' He calls Peter and puts his hand on his shoulder. 'You go to bed too. I am proud of you and my family today.'

Mrs Kassis discards her tea towel and starts walking towards the bedroom. Quietly she speaks to her daughter. 'Tessa, you are so important to my life.' Cold shivers run down Tessa's back as she feels the responsibility for her mother's happiness. Her mother is fragile, like translucent glass. Tessa puts her arms around her.

The house has settled when Tessa knocks on Peter's door. 'Come in.'

Tessa pushes open the door to see him standing in his navy checked flannel pyjamas. Glancing around his room, she smiles at the rugby pennants stuck on the wall and the weights in the corner and the dirty shirts clinging to his cupboard. 'I bought this specially for your graduation.' He unwraps the brown paper. As he opens it, shadowed light reflects from the silver. He traces the engravings with his fingers and Tessa touches his hand. 'I want you to like it.'

'I do.' He smiles. 'Tessa, even though you're a pain sometimes, I'm glad you're my sister.'

She hugs her brother.

***

The next weeks are silent, intense as Peter studies for his public examinations and Tessa studies for her finals. The creative writing meetings have come to an end for the year and the focus is on studying. In the library, Jenny and Tessa review their work. Jenny doesn't see James for a few weeks. There's relief for Tessa as the exams force thoughts of David, into the back room of her mind.

Mr and Mrs Kassis leave their children to study. They settle into a routine of meals and retirement to their rooms. From her window, Tessa watches curiously as her father runs his rough hands against the bark of the trees. He pumps mist over the leaves to protect the trees against the summer insects, that attack the emerging fruits and flowers.

Peter is tense when the actual weeks of exams commence, but Tessa has a new confidence since university. She slips the lunch of olives, tomatoes and fresh bread her mother prepares in her bag, as she leaves with her brother for the bus stop.

'Don't be nervous, Peter. Just write what you know. You're clever. You'll do really well in the exams.'

He shakes his head. 'Maybe.'

Throughout the exams, they walk to the bus stop together. At the end of every day, they talk about the questions and answers until insecurities fade and they go to their rooms feeling calm.

Finally, exams are over. The household goes back to normal. Peter helps in his father's factory. Tessa helps her mother in the house.

Peter throws a kumquat at Tessa who's cutting carnations in the garden for the house.

'Missed.' She laughs mercilessly, throwing three kumquats back at him. Little orange balls squish and squash between roses and lemon trees. Mrs Kassis runs out of the house. 'Children, my jam. My jam. Stop it. Stop it.' Peter can't stop one that's already in orbit. It hits his mother on the head, splattering over her tidy bun. Even though her mother looks sad, Tessa can't stop giggling.

When Tessa calms down she apologises and Peter collects kumquats for his mother 's jam. Mrs Kassis is appeased and goes back into the kitchen to prepare the special jam to be sold to raise more money for the Greek school.

***

Exciting news. Athena 's coming home. Mr Kassis is too busy at work to take Tessa to meet her at the airport, so she waits by the phone. Her mother is talking to a friend about the Greek Young Matrons' Ball. Tessa watches the hands of her wristwatch tick forward, watches her mother's lips move over imperfect teeth. Ten minutes. Twelve minutes. Fifteen minutes.

Shut up. Just shut up. But her mother is excited about the ball and her kumquats. 'They are bitter. So, do you think it will make nice jam?' She puts down the phone, nearly bumping into Tessa. 'I did not see you there.'

The phone rings. 'Tessa, is that you? I'm back.' *Back, back. Athena is here.* They talk quickly, but parents and relatives interrupt her as she tries to squeeze Christos and journalism and Greece into five minutes.

'I give up. Tessa, we'll see each other tomorrow.'

'Where?'

'The front lawn at the university at ten o'clock.'

Over dinner Mr Kassis asks her about Athena.

'We're meeting tomorrow.'

He eats the black olives Mrs Kassis has laid on his plate. 'You must ask her to visit us.'

The next day Tessa stands waiting on the lawn in a printed floral dress that catches in the breeze. Now that university exams are over, there's a final meeting of the Student's Women's Lobby. Students are carrying banners. 'Life Wasn't Meant to Be Easy', 'Not Good Enough'. Usually Tessa would be interested, but not now. Nervously she looks for Athena in the growing crowds. Suddenly Athena's arms are around her and they hug between the students and the posters. There's no awkwardness, no memories forgotten, just happiness at seeing each other.

They walk through the university grounds because Tessa wants to show Athena everything. David's rooms, The Pit, her first lecture hall, the gardens and the life that Athena hasn't shared with her. It's afternoon when they leave the university to walk along the narrow roads. 'They're like the streets around our school.' They share school memories. 'It seems ages ago.'

They enter a small terrace with vines winding between the latticework of the balcony and sit on wooden chairs by a window that overlooks the street.

The smell of coffee is strong, enticing as they drink cappuccino and eat raisin toast.

Athena tells her about a temple commanding views over the Mediterranean and climbing the mountain of Delphi where she saw gods, and small villages by the edges of the sea, with fishermen catching octopus and silver fish.

'Is it always so beautiful, Athena?'

'No, not always.' Athena drinks her coffee. 'There are awful industrial areas on the outskirts of Athens, with people living in apartment blocks that would be condemned here.' She shakes her head. 'But what's really awful are the women in Athens who dye their hair so that they're blonde. They still look like women from Greece and the black roots of their hair finger to the surface. I don't have to do that. I'm allowed to have dark hair because I'm not born there.' Athena pushes back her thick shining hair.

'Why would they do it anyway?'

'I don't know.' Athena continues. 'And the men are unfaithful and the women just pretend they don't know.' She pauses. 'I wrote to you that Christos was unfaithful.' Tessa touches Athena's hand. 'It crushed me.' Athena looks down. 'What about you and your Professor Davids?'

Tessa bites her nails.

'You haven't changed. I know it's serious if you bite your nails.'

Tessa puts down her hands. 'Yes, it was serious, for me anyway. He hasn't even written to me. And he promised.'

'Men can be liars.'

'Not David. He's not.'

'All right, he's not. Sorry Tessa, I've become sceptical.'

They order more cappuccino and raisin toast.

'I love David'. She holds her coffee cup, feeling its warmth. 'We made love. Well, nearly. I wanted to. I didn't care about my father or the Church or if I'd I go to hell.'

'Hell? I don't think so Tessa.'

'Well, it was David who wouldn't. I guess he was right. I don 't know. I miss him so much. It hurts.' They sit quietly looking out of the cafe window into the street, watching students walking towards the train station.

'I made love with Christos. My only love. Once, one of my father's friends pushed me against the wall of my house and touched me. It was disgusting, but Christos was different. He was beautiful and his hands were beautiful.' Athena pauses. 'You're right. The betrayal hurts.'

Arm in arm, they walk to the bus like schoolgirls. 'Athena, you know the Greek Young Matrons' Ball?' Athena nods. 'Well, I know you hate it, and so do I, but my parents are forcing me to go. Will. you come with me? You can sit at our table.'

'Tessa, that's a huge favour.' 'Oh. If it's too much then...'

'Just joking. Of course I'll come.'

Tessa gets off the bus and walks towards her house. *Athena. Athena. You're home.*

Chapter 16

'I won't. I won't.'

'But it is so lovely.' Mrs Kassis pleads with her daughter in the dressing room of the dress shop.

Tessa strips the white taffeta and lace off her body. 'It feels like sandpaper and I look like a cream meringue. Why don't you make me put cherries in my hair as well? I hate it.'

Mrs Kassis looks confused.

'I won't go to the stupid dance in this. I don't want to go anyway. I'm not one of the girls being presented, so why do I have to look like this?' Tessa can't stop tears. 'Go away Mama. Just go away.'

Mrs Kassis leaves the dressing room flustered.

Tessa refuses to speak to her mother, as they walk out of the shop into the street. She's silent all the way to the bus stop and on the bus as well.

'I do not understand, Tessa. I just want to buy you a lovely dress like the other girls will wear. What is wrong with this?'

'I'm not like the other girls. I'm Tessa. I'm me.' She bites her nail. 'The dress may be lovely to you, but it isn't to me. I'm nineteen going on twenty. Haven't I even the right to dress myself?'

'Your father wants... ' Mrs Kassis doesn't finish her sentence.

'I don't care what he wants. '

Mrs Kassis shakes her head. 'I wish you to be happy, Tessa. What is it you will wear?'

'A plain evening dress.' The bus jerks to a stop and they move towards the exit. 'I don't care if it's white, if that's what you expect. Just something simple with straps to hide my bra. I'm only going to the ball because you want me there. I'm sorry if I'm upsetting you, but at least I don't want to look awful.'

Mrs Kassis sighs. 'All right.' They leave the bus to walk home. Mrs Kassis occupies herself tidying her bun with its wisps of straying brown hair. Tessa sees the confusion behind her mother's busy hands and wispy hair. *I don't care. I just don't.*

Tessa is relieved when they get home and she can leave her mother thinking about dresses and the ball. She's arranged for Athena and Jenny to meet for a picnic in the park across the road. The picnic basket is already packed with fresh bread, cheese and summer fruits. Ripe yellow mangoes and reddish peaches and the big strawberries that she grows in the garden. She grabs it and heads for the park, to the sandstone obelisk, a memorial to soldiers who died in World War I.

Athena waves as she approaches the obelisk from the iron spearhead gate entrance, and Jenny waves too as she approaches the main gates. They're awkward when they first meet, and busy themselves with preparations. The rug is thrown over the grass, plates and glasses unpacked. When their picnic is laid out and they have settled onto the rug, they look at each other awkwardly, until Athena starts laughing. Then Tessa does. Then Jenny and then it's all right. Athena talks about Greece and Christos and journalism. Jenny talks about training to be a teacher and James and how much money she makes waitressing, and Tessa talks about writing and David and the Greek Young Matrons' Dinner Ball.

'I won. I'm not wearing a meringue to the dance.'

'You're peculiar, Tessa.' Jenny bites into a peach.

The juice trickles down her chin. 'And you're revolting.'

I can't help it that you brought the juiciest peach, in the whole world. It's delicious.' Jenny takes another mouthful and there're more drips.

I'm wearing a blueberry tart dress,' Athena teases. 'What's that?' Tessa and Jenny say together. 'You'll have to be there and see. Why don't you come with us, Jenny? It'll be fun with three of us.'

'I don't know.'

'Come on. You'll give James a run for his money. There'll be some gorgeous Greek guys there.' Athena laughs. 'Really cute guys.' Tessa rolls her eyes.

They harass Jenny to come to the ball.

'But I've never met your parents, Tessa. They won't know why I'm there.'

'It's not like that. You're allowed to come, since it'll be raising money for charity. I'm buying the ticket for you.'

'No. I can't let you do that, Tessa.'

'You can't let me down. Please. I want to buy your ticket. You have to come. Please?' Tessa tempts her with a sweet red strawberry. 'Here. It's one of my special strawberries that I've grown just for you. It's even juicier than the peach.'

'Bribery will get you everywhere.' Jenny bites into it, savouring the sweet pink flesh.

***

The dress for the ball is pushed into the background, as Christmas preparations take over. Biscuits have to be baked and Christmas puddings prepared. The puddings are Mrs Kassis' speciality, wrapped in cloth and tied with tinsel. Decorations have to be made as well, and there are presents to buy and wrap. Tessa loves this time with her mother, and they're like girls as they cut the cellophane.

It's been more than two months since David has written. Tessa pretends it doesn't matter, but at night she fantasises that his arms are around her and she wakes up loving the pillow. *David why don't you write? Please David, Please.* She posts David the journal with her poetry in it.

The priest honours her parents with a visit to the house. Mrs Kassis and Tessa lay out the dolmades, taramasalata and spinach squares on the coffee table in the sitting room. The priest is punctual. His long black flowing gown and dark beard are familiar and Mr Kassis welcomes him into his house.

The priest is a stern man, unwilling to compromise on the stringent morals of his Church. Around him, Tessa is nervous, and she hopes he doesn't sense her other life, hidden behind her serving. The priest compliments Mrs Kassis on her dolmades, making her smile. Mr Kassis and the priest talk politics and social order while Peter listens respectfully, speaking only when a question is directed at him.

The women clear the table and bring the cakes they have spent days preparing. Tessa licks honey from her fingers as she carries sweet baklava laden with honey and nuts to the table. Almond pastries, Greek sweets, kataifi lie on the table like wanton women ready to be taken. Tessa smiles as the priest and her father being wrapped around the pastries.

The priest leaves, content. Mr Kassis goes to his room, because he is tired from the long hours in his factory. Peter sees that his mother is tired too, and takes some plates to the kitchen to help her. Mrs Kassis kisses her son. Tessa and her mother continue cooking and baking for the events that mark the visiting and feasting of Christmas.

***

A letter from David.

Dear Tessa

I received your poetry. Thank you. It's special. Don't be angry at me for not writing sooner, but there are excuses that I won't give you. I wasn't sure if I should write at all, but memories of the last weeks we spent together filter into my thoughts while I work at my books. I miss you and our games with the poets. I think about you often.

Cambridge is cold and white. A cover of light snow and rain drizzles over the town making it misty, undefined. People slip and fall. I have to hide behind a woollen scarf when I run across the commons to the university.

Its beautiful, old, and when the wind becomes biting I go through the grounds and look for all those things we found together in the hot Australian sun in our university.

They think I'm mad here, which I enjoy immensely. They accept it because I'm a colonial affected by the sun. I have to wear my black graduate cloak and as I charge through the long open corridors the cloak billows around me. The students seem to find me strange.

Sometimes they jump when I demand an answer, a thought. Then I remember you jumping too and how your mind surprised me.

I've found the archives inspiring. There are original books by scholars of the past and intricately drawn dramatizations of their work. Their appeal is lessened without you and I feel irrationally angry at you for not being here to help me.

Cambridge is important to me, but I'm relieved not to be involved in university politics here. I'm too unconventional for them to even worry about me. I will finish my book here but I'm coming back during the Christmas break for a few weeks and I will see you then. It seems a long time.

Love David

Tessa throws the letter onto her bed. *How could you leave me waiting, just waiting, when I miss you so much? How, David?* She grabs the letter and throws the pages into the air, watching them waft to her bedroom floor. The papers lie still on the floral carpet. She bends to pick them up, pressing them against her. *I love you.*

Tessa shares the letter with Athena. 'You see, I was right.'

'It's hard, Athena.'

'Relationships are hard. Christos hasn't written either.' They hug each other.

'It's easier when you're here, Athena.'

'That's the same for me.'

***

The Greek Young Matrons' Ball arrives. 'You look I gorgeous, Peter.' Tessa straightens his purple bow tie. 'And so do you.' Tessa has let her hair out, leaving the dark curls to dance softly around her face. Her long cream satin dress is different to her usual pleats and jumpers. She wears pale rose satin gloves that rise to her elbows.

Mrs Kassis clasps her gold chain with a pearl drop around Tessa's neck. 'Your father bought this for me, when I married. I want to give it to you now. One day it will be your time to marry.'

'One day.' Tessa hugs her mother. 'Thank you.'

Mr Kassis strides into the sitting room, surveys his family. He looks at Tessa, who lifts her chin as if in defiance. 'You are beautiful tonight, Tessa.' He pats her cheek. 'Who would believe this? It is such a long way from the village of my boyhood.' He takes her hand. 'We will go now.'

The hotel is ablaze with lights. The red carpet marks their way to the ballroom, as penguin coated men gather with their wives and daughters, birds of paradise for the display of success that has followed migration and years of hard work.

Athena and Jenny run to Tessa as she enters. The three girls hold onto to one another, giggling, until Mr Kassis interrupts, amused. Athena is startling in her blueberry chiffon. It clings to her, making her skin white like alabaster and her lips crimson like sunrise. Mr Kassis greets her and Jenny. Jenny's blonde hair and summer yellow complete the balance, as they breeze through the ballroom.

When everyone is seated, the Archbishop opens the proceedings. 'I congratulate the Greek Young Matrons' Association for the remarkable philanthropic work it does for Greek Australians and the community at large.

I pray that God will richly bless all your future endeavours.'

Everyone claps, while Athena looks around to see who's there. She points out the handsomest men in the room. They watch the meringues, partnered by pimpled boys, walking down the aisle like brides to be presented to the Mayor. Tessa whispers. They look nice but I'm relieved it's not me.' Every dress gets an analysis and a number out of ten. Parents and relatives clap. Mothers look on anxiously, hoping that their creations are the best.

The parents approve the Mayor's speech. 'The pride and love of family and friends is surpassed only by the beauty and grace of the lovely debutantes. You will always remember this night.

I am sure that each of you appreciate the love, guidance and direction given to you by your parents during your formative years and I wish you every success and happiness.'

Tessa sneaks a look at her father, who's nodding agreement. Athena smiles behind her hand like she does in Sunday service. Jenny has a giggling fit, which she tries to gag with her serviette.

After the speeches and main courses, there is dancing. Girls in white and their partners twirl around the room as if in a traditional wedding waltz. Then the real dancing starts. Athena grabs Tessa's hand and Tessa grabs Jenny's and they join the circle. Tessa notices John Pappas on the other side, looking handsome in his dark suit and white embroidered shirt. He acknowledges her and she smiles back. The music starts. It's slow at first. Jenny copies Tessa in repetitive steps of kicking and turning. 'You're dancing the Kalomatyano. We always dance it.'

'I love it.' Jenny is concentrating hard on copying Tessa's feet.

Mr and Mrs Kassis join the girls as the music beats rhythmically, and as past traditions vibrate between chandeliers and magnificent floral arrangements. The dancers bend and kick, coasting around the sparkling ballroom, quickening as the beat becomes more insistent and the rhythm more compelling. Dancing until there's laughing and wildness, until the chandeliers are irrelevant and grandmas and mothers and children are all clapping and pounding the passions of past lives. And it's Zorba dancing on the beach, and Athena stopping for breath hugging Jenny, and John Pappas laughing as he twirls Tessa around the floor, and Mr Kassis holding Mrs Kassis like she's a girl again.

Chapter 17

Jenny and her family are spending Christmas with her grandparents in the country. Tessa is amazed that James is going with them. 'How come your parents don't mind? You're not marrying him, are you?'

'Tessa, do you mind? He's just a friend. Well, I like him a lot. That's all.' Jenny wrinkles her nose. 'One day I want to get married and have kids. Not now, of course. Don't you? '

'I don't know.' Tessa touches the top of Jenny's head. 'I wish you hadn't cut off all your hair.'

'Don't you like my blonde fuzz?'

Tessa gives her a huge floppy hat for Christmas. To protect your head. It matches your blue eyes as well.' Jenny pulls her hat on. 'I love it. I love it. It's perfect for the boiling hot Christmas we're going to have in Bathurst.'

Jenny hands Tessa a package. 'I've been dying to give this to you. I found this shop that you 'd go mad in, Tessa. I went mad myself and bought you lots.' Tessa can't believe it, so many exotic shells with spikes and smoothness and colours. Jenny concentrates as she recites their names and natural habitats.

South African Turban from South Africa. That's pretty obvious.' She laughs. 'Here's a Chequered Bonnet!' You can find it in sandy mud in the Indo-Pacific, and the Blistered Margin Shell is found in the Caribbean.' Jenny goes on and on until she completes her list and Tessa's laughing.

'You're so clever, Jenny.'

'I'll see you when uni starts again.' Jenny pats her hat. 'Don't have too much fun without me.'

'Sure, as if that's likely.'

A letter is waiting for Tessa at home. She tears open the envelope and finds two tickets and a scribbled note.

You have to come to my first official performance. It's a send up of Hamlet at the university theatre. I'm Hamlet of course. Hope you cart bear one of your heroes getting a little sticky. You have to come.

Remember. Support your writing group!

Joel

Tessa looks at the tickets. Jen*ny's right, I'm going to have fun. I'll ask Athena. I just have to weave threads around my father.*

That night when Mr Kassis is relaxing in his armchair after his meal, when Mrs Kassis is quietly wrapping puddings with cloth and ribbon, when Peter is reading the newspaper, Tessa talks to her father about the Shakespearian drama she has been studying.

'When we are born, we cry that we are come to this great stage of fools. King Lear was such a fool, Papa. He listened to the daughters who told him what he wanted to hear and rejected the honest daughter because she wouldn't lie.'

'It is very difficult to really listen.' Mr Kassis presses tobacco into his pipe. 'We all are prejudiced by our own experiences, our own beliefs about ourselves. How could King Lear really believe his older daughters when they said they loved him more than 'eyesight, space and liberty'?'

'I wouldn't voluntarily blind myself because I love you, Papa.'

146

Mr Kassis smiles. 'I hope you would not. I would not want you to be blind or to have anything but the very best for you.' He lights his pipe. 'This King Lear is a fool because he wants everyone to praise him. Words are cheap. It is how you behave that matters.' Smoke from his pipe wafts through the room. 'There are never easy answers. King Lear had a kingdom which gave him power, but with that came responsibility. You cannot have one without the other. He took what looked the easy way. Give up responsibility but still be king. For this great mistake, he lost his kingdom, his family, friends and, in the end, his life.'

Mrs Kassis enjoys listening to her husband and daughter. She interrupts to bring them coffee. As she puts down Mr Kassis' cup, he presses her hand. 'Thank you. The coffee smells very good.'

Tessa sips coffee. 'Students are putting on a local version of Hamlet at university. I've been given tickets for Athena and me. I'd really like to see it. Can I go, Papa?'

Before Mr Kassis can answer, Tessa adds, 'If Peter drives us there and collects us, it'll be all right, won't it?' Tessa turns to Peter, who's put down the newspaper. He shakes his head. 'See, Peter wants to take us.'

Mr Kassis laughs. 'All right, all right, if your brother takes you, you can go.' !

'Thank you, thank you.' Mr Kassis enjoys Tessa's excitement. 'Peter, you're the best brother.' He groans.

Peter is in a good mood when he drives Athena and Tessa to the theatre. He's meeting his friends at the uni pub for a drink while the girls watch Hamlet. Athena buys chocolate-covered almonds in the foyer before they go inside. Carol is already sitting in the front row. Tessa introduces Athena to her. After the introduction, Carol dives into what she's involved in now. 'It's just been established. A feminist press. It's a collective and everyone works for free until we make money, if we ever do. Come along. Jenny and Athena can come too.'

Athena's interested but Tessa shakes her head. 'I've got enough problems just getting to this.'

'Shush.' Jenny pulls Tessa's sleeve. The curtain rises. Carol rolls her eyes at the gawky stage craft. She whispers. 'Are they Joel's underpants hanging on the tree?' They giggle. Tessa points Joel out to Athena when he appears.

'Cute,' Athena observes.

The audience is rolling in the aisles by the time Joel has killed himself with a rubber dagger. There's applause and cheering. Tessa says to Athena; 'I don't think this would be my father's idea of Shakespeare.' There are dozens of curtain calls, with people shouting for Joel. He bows and waves, then winks at Tessa. Athena nudges Tessa. 'What's that about?'

'Nothing.' Tessa blushes as they make their way backstage, where Joel has his arm around a pretty girl in jeans and a see-through top. 'See, Joel means nothing, I told you.'

Carol calls out, 'You haven 't changed, Joel.'

'You were terrific, Joel.' He puts his other arm around Tessa before she slides away, to join Athena in the crowd of students and friends.

Tessa says wryly to Athena, 'Joel was nearly a mistake.'

'You'll have to explain that one.'

'I got caught up with his acting once, that's all.'

'Sometimes men just play with us like we're toys, says Shakespeare.' Athena watches Joel charm the girls.

'Well, Joel does in any case.'

Peter is waiting outside. As they pile into the car, Peter shakes his head. 'I expect you all want lifts home?'

'Of course.' Tessa taps his shoulder. 'Drive on.'

***

Christmas starts in earnest for the Kassis family. There is the fast before the service. Tessa helps her mother with the final decorations for the Christmas table. She enjoys curling the satin ribbons and hanging the baubles on the tree in the sitting room. Her father cuts a branch from the giant fir in their garden, making the house fragrant with mountain scent.

Tessa goes to bed hungry. She tries to concentrate on her faith. She wants to be penitent, to remember her sins and seek forgiveness. Instead she sleeps restlessly, as images of Joel's tricks wrestle with the sterility of white rooms and King Lear's broken face. She settles momentarily, feeling David's body beside her, tasting his mouth against her, until shadows with black robes unsettle her again, darkening her dreams. She wakes, sucking her fingers.

It seems like night when she gets up. Quietly, the family dress in the dark. They are always one of the first at the service. It's four in the morning as they enter the church. Tessa feels the acid from hunger pangs. Mr Kassis lights a candle, placing it before the embossed icon of Jesus. Then they light candles, making the glow from the fire light Christ's face, and Tessa thinks of a soft baby like in Christmas card pictures. She kneels to

149

recite the prayers she says, every Christmas. She listens to the chanting, she hears every Christmas. The incense wafts between the words and her thoughts. She focuses on the altar, where the Virgin Mary offers intervention for man's salvation. She hears her father murmur prayers to the Virgin and her mother give thanks.

Tessa jerks her head upright. She squints at her parents. What is it? There's incongruity. She shakes her head because she wants the incongruity to disappear. It doesn't. 'Go away,' she whispers urgently, kneeling on the hard-wooden planks. But the questions pulsate from the altar, like they have a life of their own. *Why do men pray to the mother of Christ? Women praise a mother too, but isn't Mary a woman, like me, like my mother, like Athena? Would the priest or my father listen to Mary today in this church if she sat beside them as a woman, as a mother?*

Athena is late and soundlessly kneels next to her. She puts her hand over Tessa's, who closes her eyes tight. Men worship Mary's virginity - the creation of the baby God without a man. *Mary's bypassed them. God's her lover. Is that why they guard so jealously the chastity of young girls? Is that why men want it? Does it make them gods? But then, after that, what are women? Whores? Madonnas?*

The incense is sweet, delicious. Tessa breathes it, wanting to shut out blasphemous thoughts. She opens her eyes to Athena and presses against her. She wants the clarity of faith, but sees it dripping like melted wax into pools of formless shapes.

The service ends and she walks hand in hand with Athena down the centre aisle, past friends and relatives.

John Pappas nods at her. Outside the fresh air clears the incense. Athena leaves Tessa, to go with her own family to celebrate.

The Kassis family drinks coffee and eats lightly. Mr Kassis talks to Peter about business. Tessa and Mrs Kassis make the last preparations for the meal. Traditional pork - heavy, succulent - lies on the central platter. The table is festive, the food plentiful and Mrs Kassis happy.

The godchildren come. Mrs Kassis gives them the special Christmas bread she's made, covered in white powdery sugar. The children play with the small ornaments Mrs Kassis has carefully attached to the bread, and she watches as they search for the coins hidden in the bottom of the bread.

***

There are visits and celebrations and the presents of the New Year.

Peter is relieved when he's offered a place in the law faculty. Tessa is offered a place in the honours class. Mr Kassis looks at his children over breakfast. He nods, '1978 will be a good year.' Tessa butters her bread. She has heard on the radio this morning that statistics indicate nearly 66 per cent of Australian women will be working in paid employment by 1990.

She watches her mother shape and reshape the bread piled on the table, cutting more slices as bread is eaten, cutting more slices so that there is plenty of bread.

Chapter 18

Tessa, Athena and Jenny run towards each other on the front lawn of the university. They grab hands. Dark and black and blonde hair intermingle, as they spin around toppling onto the summer grass. 'I had the best Christmas. The best.' Jenny's breathless.

Athena lies on her back. 'Tell us all about it.' Tessa sits cross-legged between them.

'You've got to promise to think it's wonderful.' Athena and Tessa smile. 'It's James. He's different to any other guy I've gone out with. We're friends as well.' Jenny talks about early morning rides through the bush, lying in the cold river water when the sun is burning, hiking up the mountain at the back of the property. 'We could see the whole world from the top.' She stops. 'Well, we felt we could.' She rubs her hair, which is a bit longer now. 'It's real.' Memories of liquidambar trees and white coats and Jenny, make Tessa bite' her lip. 'I love James.'

Tessa pulls at the lime green shoots and forces a smile. *Love. I don't understand love.* Every day she goes to her letterbox. Sometimes she walks slowly, imagining that if she's slow enough, there will be time for David's letter to arrive. Sometimes she runs, panting, driving her hand into the opening, reaching for envelopes with only Mr Kassis' name. Every day she writes to David, about her family, her writing, her friends, her thoughts. But she doesn't send the letters.

'Love is wonderful.' Athena thinks of Christos. 'Just be careful.'

***

Saturday afternoon. Mrs Kassis waits nervously in the kitchen for Tessa to come in from the garden. She has set the table with a pot of tea, two cups and saucers and small china plates. Tessa arrives with pink roses. 'Mama, you have to smell the roses. They're so sweet.' Tessa notices almond biscuits. 'You spoil me.' She gives the flowers to her mother, while she fills a crystal vase with water. Then she puts each rose separately into the water, stripping excess leaves, leaving thorns and petals. 'Beautiful, aren't they?'

Mrs Kassis pours tea for her daughter and herself. 'Sit down Tessa. Have your tea and biscuits.' Tessa bites into the almond shortbread.

Mrs Kassis drinks her tea slowly, nervously. She puts down her cup and fiddles with her teaspoon. 'Your father wants to speak to you after his work today.'

'Yes.' Tessa takes another bite of the biscuit. 'You are definitely the best cook in the world.'

Mrs Kassis murmurs. 'It's time you know.'

'What should I know?' Tessa finishes the biscuit.

'You'll be twenty soon.'

Tessa' teases. 'Are you giving me a party? If you are, Athena and Jenny have to come.'

Mrs Kassis is confused. 'Athena? Jenny? Yes, they are nice girls. A party? Would you like a celebration?' She puts down her teaspoon. 'We could have one with the family. Yes, and the girls could come.'

'No, it's fine. I'm joking. Anyway, my birthday's ages away'

Mrs Kassis continues. 'You'll be finishing your degree next year.'

153

Tessa interrupts. 'Peter has five years to go to finish law. That seems so long. I'm glad I'm not doing it.' She takes another almond biscuit. 'Athena likes university. She's going to do really well. Papa said Athena can visit. Can she?'

'Yes, Tessa, but... '

Tessa doesn't let her mother finish. 'I have to do an honours year and,' Tessa hesitates, 'if I'm good enough, I want to do my masters. Maybe I'll specialise in D. H. Lawrence. I really love the course I'm doing now on his writing.'

Mrs Kassis shakes her head. 'You are mixing me up. Can you listen to me?' Tessa stops. 'Your father is to talk to you.'

'Yes, you've told me already; Tonight.'

'Tessa, your father will explain.' Mrs Kassis moves the biscuit crumbs on her plate from side to side. 'You can choose others of course. This is not like at home. I could not choose. But to begin, your father has two men from old families. You can choose. You know them.' Mrs Kassis does not look at her daughter.

Tessa stares at her mother. 'What are you talking about?'

'You know what it is.'

'I don't.'

'It will soon be time,' Mrs Kassis pauses, 'to arrange, who you will marry.'

Tessa stands up from the table. This is ridiculous.'

Mrs Kassis fumbles with her chair and follows her daughter. 'It will be all right, Tessa. It is for you to choose.'

'I chose no one then.'

Mrs Kassis holds her arm. 'It will be all right.'

Tessa pushes her away. 'Are you alright?' Her mother puts her hands across her mouth. 'You know I have things I want to do. You know that.' She stares at her mother. 'Do you want me to get married, when I don't want to be married? I'm not even twenty. I'm just finding out who I am. I don't even know if I like myself yet. How can I be a wife, when I don't feel like a person yet?'

Mrs Kassis' voice is muffled behind her hands. 'I just want to tell you. Do you understand, you can choose? There are two to choose from.' Tessa paces the kitchen.

'Choose? I won't. I won't be like you. I won't.'

Mrs Kassis stretches out her arms to Tessa, but she turns away. She runs out of the kitchen, outside the house, across the road, into the park. She runs until she's panting. She runs until she can't run anymore. *They can't make me. They can't.*

She breathes heavily at first, then more lightly, sensing the trees moving in the wind, the ducks landing on the lake. Slowly she starts moving again. She sees the familiar memorial made of sandstone and makes her way to it. There are lists of names in alphabetical order. John Anthony Coleman, Paul Thomas Coates, Samuel Henry Day... lists that go on to O'Malley and Ryan and Thompson. Anglo- Saxon names, not foreign like her own. But she feels Australian. She touches the rough sandstone and rests her head against the names of young men who died in World War I, a long time ago, when they were Tessa's age. Everyone ending as dust like the Bible says. She sits by the memorial and digs her fingers into the wet grass, trying to understand the point. The soldiers died for Australia. Jenny 's baby is already becoming dust. A short journey from creation to cessation. There has to be a point to living. *What is it? What?*

She thinks of her mother waiting for her in the kitchen. *I love you so much, but I just can't.* Tessa cries, leaning against the names of young Australian men etched in sandstone.

The afternoon darkens into evening and she knows she has to go back. She stands up and stares across the park to see her home in the distance. She forces her feet back, each step exhausting her. She imagines her father sitting in his armchair reading his paper, her mother furtively cooking the evening meal, Peter listening to his Beethoven tape in his room.

She pushes open the back door. Mrs Kassis is waiting for her. They don't speak. Mr Kassis calls Tessa to the sitting room. Peter's just come into the room and is pulling out a chair. Mrs Kassis follows Tessa and sits in the corner, where she takes needle and thread to mend socks and shirts. Tessa watches her and wonders why her mother isn't the paint on the wall or the chair. Then she could be totally nothing at all.

Mr Kassis enjoys his family being together in the room. It reminds him of evenings, when he was a boy. Slowly he pushes the tobacco in his pipe with his thumb, yellowed with practice. He lights a match and puffs until the tobacco is burning. He smiles at Tessa. She's a good daughter and she's done well for him at university. He feels a momentary sadness at the thought that she will leave his house one day. He'll miss her cleverness and laughter. He'll miss those times, when she sits at his feet and listens to his stories.

He waves his hand, directing her to the floral settee. 'Sit down Tessa.'

She can choose between two good men. Either will look after her and her children. There will be grandchildren. He enjoys that thought. 'I understand that your mother has told you. You must think of marriage.' Tessa looks at her mother mending Peter's shirt. 'John Pappas will be visiting in a week, on Saturday. Paul Couris will come another time. I want you to choose. They have both asked about you. You are popular, Tessa.'

Tessa shudders. John Pappas who doesn't speak to her, whose mother's face crepes into frowns and dissatisfaction. Paul Couris whose father does business with her father. *Who are they? Why can't you let me find out who I am? Why can't I really choose? I hate you.* 'But it's too soon. I have to finish university.'

He agrees. 'It is not straight away.'

I hate you, Papa. 'I'd like to do more study.'

'Yes, you will do your librarian diploma. A good profession for marriage.'

I hate you. 'I'm not ready to get married yet. I don't know how to be married.'

'You will learn, Tessa.'

She wants to vomit, like when she heard Miss Newland crying in the toilet. 'I'm not ready, Father.'

'It is decided.'

She closes her eyes, blocking out his pipe and thick fisherman's hands. 'Don't make me, Papa.'

Mr Kassis puts down his pipe. 'I know, what is right.'

She opens her eyes. 'Do you?'

'You will do as I say. I am your father and know what is right.'

Athena, are you here? Help me. Please. Tessa stands up. 'I can't, Papa.'

Her mother is mouthing words at her, to stop.

'It is enough.' Her father gets up from his armchair. Peter shifts uncomfortably. Mrs Kassis stops mending.

'I won't, Father.'

His legs are astride and his hands outstretched. 'What have you learnt in this house, in our church?'

She hesitates. 'But this isn't to do with this house or the Church or God.'

Mr Kassis walks over to Tessa. He takes her chin, forcing her face up. 'Stop this, Tessa.'

Her mouth is dry. She swallows, then answers with as much force as she can. 'No. I will not do as you say.'

He waits a moment. Stares at his daughter.

'I will not, Father.' She stares back defiantly.

He raises his hand instinctively. She does not shield her face, as he strikes her with his open palm.

Mrs Kassis jumps up from her seat. Tessa does not cry.

'You will see John Pappas on Saturday.'

Chapter 19

i'm stuck in a mirror
they see, but
i'm invisible
softly splitting
grey matter into
nose
eyes
toes

Tessa puts her pen down, to stroke the blue porcelain duck from the fete. She had forgotten to give it to Athena and now it's too used to her desk and the trees it sees from the window. *You can't leave me, can you?* Tessa moves away from her desk, undressing automatically, leaving her clothes lying haphazardly on the floral carpet. She switches off the light, then climbs into bed. Lying very still under the sheets, she waits for sleep. But there is no sleep as she stares into darkness, as the tears roll down her face, as the night waits for light.

Tessa dresses for church and pads quietly down the stairs to the kitchen. Mrs Kassis is waiting. 'I have boiled water for your tea.'

Tessa shakes her head. 'How could you, Mama?' Mrs Kassis avoids her daughter's eyes. Tessa refuses the tea, leaving the room before her father comes down for his breakfast.

She says nothing in the car as Mr Kassis drives the family to the morning church service. She says nothing as she kneels in a wooden pew. Athena isn't at church.

Peter sits uneasily beside her. Tessa refuses to look at her father.

***

Monday. Tessa meets Athena in the library. She listens to her talk about an offer to work on the Athens newspaper over Christmas. 'It's ages away, but I've got to make a decision now.' Athena takes a book from a shelf. 'Christos could be there. I don't know if I could cope with seeing him.' They move towards a table. 'I wish I'd never met him. I don't think I can go.'

Tessa doesn't respond, as they lay out their pens and paper ready to research and study. They pull out their chairs lo sit down. Athena turns the pages of the book restlessly. Tessa's voice is unsteady. 'Why should you decide to go or stay, because of Christos? Do you think that's what he does?'

'I suppose he doesn't.'

He's lucky to have even known you, and you loved him too.' She waits for a moment. 'Christos abused you.' Athena rubs her eyes, but Tessa doesn't comfort her. 'He hurt you. Are you going to let him hurt you even more?'

The murmur of students and books hums between the desks and their words. Athena leans over the table towards Tessa. 'I'll go to Greece at Christmas.' Athena pauses. 'But you have to come with me. Will you come with me?'

Tessa touches her cheek as if it's still stinging from her father's hand. 'Yes.'

They study until lunchtime, when they collect their books and walk to the cafeteria to. meet Jenny. It's crowded but Jenny has saved a table outside for them.

160

Jenny talks about her essay on educational psychology. 'It's interesting. I think I'll like being a teacher, if I ever get through.'

Athena smiles. 'You'll have to spend less time with James then.'

'Very funny.' Jenny bites into her salad sandwich.

'Well, we've got exciting news. It might be even more exciting than James.' Athena winks. 'We're going to the Greek Islands at Christmas.'

'Lucky you.'

Athena's voice is musical. 'We're going to stroll on white sands looking fantastic, and when we're tired we'll rest against stony cliffs watching blue skies.'

Tessa looks up at the blue sky. 'We can hire a wooden boat with white billowing sails. I've seen them on postcards.'

'And dive from the boat into the cool Mediterranean waters.' Athena pretends to dive.

'And swim with fishes,' Tessa smiles, 'and mermaids.' Tessa and Athena throw images across the salad sandwiches and laminex table until the images seem real and they are there. Jenny stops eating her sandwich and adds to their game. 'And we could throw plates into the fire. I've seen that on TV.'

'Yes, we can do that if you want, Jenny. So, are you coming with us? Three travellers abroad discovering unchartered waters. Girls looking for adventure. That'll be us.' Athena beckons Jenny.

Jenny laughs. 'Okay. I'll be one of the explorers.'

'What about James? Will he survive?'

Jenny thinks for a moment.

'He can't come with us, you know.' Tessa is serious.

'I suppose.' Jenny runs her hands through her hair. 'Yes, I'm coming.'

Tessa pretends that her father never struck her face, pretends that John Pappas and Paul Couris will not court her, pretends she's already running along white sands with Athena and Jenny.

***

Saturday afternoon. John Pappas is a handsome man. He sits firmly planted in a chair watching silently as Mrs Kassis and Tessa serve coffee and cake. He only speaks when Mr Kassis asks about cars. He's nervous and there's sweat on his forehead. Tessa stares through the window and smiles at a harum-scarum girl chasing her dog. A golden Labrador. Tessa always wanted a dog and to be a harum-scarum girl.

The afternoon is long. Tessa watches the sitting room clock. She examines John Pappas. He's a few years older than David. Taller, bigger. His dark hair is neatly cut and he's cleanly shaven. No moustache. Her father has told her that his motor mechanic garage is successful. He employs five men. She notices John Pappas's hands. They are thick, roughened by heavy work. Tessa shudders at the thought of calloused hands against her skin. There is blackness under his nails. Not that he is dirty, but the oil and grease of his work isn't easily washed away.

Tessa suddenly interrupts the conversation between the men. 'Do you like your work?'

Her father smiles. 'Yes.'

'What type of cars do you repair?'

'All kinds.'

Tessa questions and he answers in monosyllables, because he's uncomfortable and not used to courting. He's glad she's talking to him until she stops, bored by his lack of communication. The afternoon ends and John Pappas promises to come again.

John Pappas lives with his parents in a large modern house. He's bought a house near them which he's renting out until he marries. Mr Kassis drives past John Pappas's house to show Tessa. White artificial Corinthian columns, hold up expansive balconies. Modern windows display a billiard table that has been cemented into the floor in the front room. Next to the house are other houses. The same. Enormous homes with sudden, raw references to other cultures attached disjointedly to their architecture.

Mr Kassis glances at Tessa, then rubs his hand as if it hurts him. He says that he'd be proud of Tessa living in that white mausoleum, encased in an enclave of other mausoleums with no park within strolling distance. There are no trees, no special hideaways. There would just be John Pappas. Tessa doesn't talk to her father. She hasn't really spoken to him since that evening he struck her.

John Pappas is to visit every Saturday and Tessa is to sit with him and eat Mrs Kassis' cakes and biscuits. Tessa hopes he sweats less and that the Saturday visits will go on forever so that she won't have to commit to him.

Athena is finally coming for dinner. She's staying the night as well. After university they walk towards Tessa's house. 'Athena, you know how I promised I'd go to

Greece with you? Well, it's not that easy. I want to go, but... '

'You have to come. You promised.'

'I don't know if my father will let me.'

Athena understands. 'Well, we'll just have to persuade him.'

That won't be easy.'

Athena puts her arm through Tessa's. 'You need to see your relatives, don't you?'

'What?' Tessa creases her forehead.

'You want to see where your father grew up, don't you?'

'I suppose I do.'

'It's important to establish your Greek cultural background. Right?'

Tessa smiles. 'Of course.'

'You'll see. We'll persuade your father.'

Mr Kassis is waiting for them in the sitting room. He's in his usual chair and Tessa remembers a long time ago, when he sat on the floral settee. Athena breezes into the room, bringing freshness into the formality of the arranged furniture and polished silver. Mrs Kassis follows them, wiping her floured hands with a tea towel. 'Dinner will be soon. How are your parents?'

'They're well.' Mrs Kassis scurries away after Athena has given her the obligatory answer.

Peter bangs the front door and they hear him slinging down his bag. 'Constitutional law is the worst.' He calls out to his mother, 'What's for dinner?'

'Souvlaki,' she answers.

'I'm starving. I need food now,' he groans.

That makes Mr Kassis smile. 'Where do you put all the food, Peter? We will have dinner after you wash and change.' Mr Kassis is amused by his son and entertained by the girls. He's also in a good mood because he's won a large order to make chairs for the hospital.

The dinner is delicious with tender lamb and white rice and feta and olive salad. Tessa picks at the food. Athena turns the conversation to Greece and how important it is to connect with her roots. I'm going back at Christmas to learn a little more about newspapers, and to see my relatives and the country. My uncle has a huge house in Athens and he's always happy if I stay there with my family or friends. You know my uncle, Mr Kassis?'

'Yes, he is a fine man.'

Athena kicks Tessa under the table. Tessa takes a breath because it's hard to talk to him. 'Papa.' Mr Kassis puts down his fork. 'I would really love to see the villages you've told me about since I was little.'

'Roots are important.'

Athena encourages Mr Kassis to reminisce and he retells the stories of his youth. 'My brother is still there and his wife and children, but many have gone to live in Athens or migrated to other countries. I would like to see Greece again.' He tears some bread. 'I have too much work in my factory.'

Athena sparkles. 'Mr Kassis, I have just thought of a wonderful idea.'

'Yes, Athena?'

'I could ask my uncle. He's your friend, so I'm sure he'd be happy about it. Why doesn't Tessa come and stay at my uncle and aunt's home in Athens at Christmas?'

Tessa coughs. 'It would be special to see Greece.'

Mr Kassis looks at his daughter whom he loves. He's sorry he hit her. 'Tessa. Let me think on it. We will see.' The coffee is strong. Enjoying his family and thoughts of Athens, Mr Kassis drinks two cups. As Tessa and Athena leave to go upstairs, he speaks slowly. 'Maybe it is a good thing, before you marry, to see where you have come from. I will write to my brother. Maybe, you can go to Greece for this holiday.'

'Thank you, Papa.'

Athena laughs as they enter Tessa's bedroom. 'See, we did it. Your father will let you go. I just know it.'

'I'm not sure.' Tessa looks out of her window towards the park. 'Come here, Athena. See, there are bats.' Black-winged creatures glide into trees. There's a large colony of them living in the park.'

Athena shivers. 'They remind me of vampires.'

'I think they're amazing.' They watch the bats as they soar and dive into the night. Turning away from the bats towards Tessa, Athena sees the trace of tears. 'You should be happy. What's wrong?'

'I should be.' Tessa closes her eyes. 'The Greek Islands will be lovely and I want... ' The words catch. Tessa's tears are quiet. Athena takes her hand, stroking her. 'Please tell me what's wrong.'

Tessa shakes her head. Gently Athena draws Tessa to the bed. They lie beside each other while Athena pulls the doona over them. It's quiet. Only the bats swish between trees and shadows. Athena asks softly, 'So what is it?'

'My father is forcing me.' Tessa hides under the doona.

'Forcing you to do what, Tessa?'

'I feel like I don't belong here. It's like my father is caught in the past, in the village he grew up in thirty years ago. Even the villages have changed, but not my father.' Tessa burrows further beneath the doona. 'He is making me get married,' she whispers, horrified. To a stranger.'

'Tessa.'

'John Pappas. Or if I don' t want him, Paul Couris or some other man.' She can hardly breathe. 'Imagine a stranger's hands touching you. Not someone I love. Like David. Not David. I'm afraid.'

Athena strokes Tessa's hair.

'John Pappas is like my father. He'll want me to be like my mother. A good wife, a good mother, a good support for his ambitions. I don't want to be that. I want to study and to write, be young, discover life.' She presses Athena's arm so tightly, she leaves red spreading patterns. 'He visits every Saturday. Last week we didn't speak.'

'You'll have to tell your father.'

'He's so strong, Athena.'

'You have to tell him.'

'I did.' Tessa whispers. 'He hit me.'

Chapter 20

Mr Kassis welcomes Paul Couris and his mother back from Greece. Paul Couris looks like John Pappas, but he doesn't have a successful mechanic's workshop which employs five men. He has a successful plumbing business, which employs two men and an apprentice. His hands are scrubbed clean. There's no oil and grease trapped under his fingernails. He has a widowed mother who comes with him when he visits Tessa. It's like the first visits with John Pappas, except he talks about Greece. Paul Couris' mother would live with them if they married. They visit Tessa on Sundays after church. '

Tessa restlessly waits for Monday. Jenny is focused on the Greek holiday and has collected pamphlets on everything from Crete to Olympus. The leaflets flap in the wind. 'Have you thought about becoming a travel agent?' Athena laughs.

'Sure,' Jenny moans. 'An exhausted travel agent.' She's working every weekend to save for the Greek holiday. James isn't impressed. I'm not available anymore, when he just feels like seeing me.' She wrinkles her nose. 'I think it's better this way.'

Athena flicks through a booklet on the Mediterranean, as they walk quickly to lectures. 'I can't wait to see it again, except this time my parents aren't paying. They're angry at me, because of Christos.' She shows Jenny a photo of a plate of octopus. 'My favourite.'

'It looks disgusting.'

'Calamari is great. Anyway, I'll make enough money for the ticket from my job. Usherette extraordinaire. It's a shame, there aren't any tips.'

'Except you get to see all the new movies.'

'A hundred times, Jenny. Not very interesting.'

The wind whips leaves about them as they hurry in different directions to their lecture rooms.

***

Saturday afternoon. John Pappas arrives. Lately, he's less awkward, less uncomfortable. He brings her chocolates and says, 'You look very pretty.' John Pappas has never complimented her before and Tessa smiles. She's used to his visits now and she tells him about her studies. She discovers that he's interested in Geography like her father. Tessa shudders. 'I don't do Geography any more,' and quickly changes the topic. He doesn't read the books Tessa reads, but he seems pleased that she is clever enough to read them.

Tessa discovers that John Pappas enjoys gardening. She shows him David's bougainvillea.

'I like trees,' he says. He grows fruit trees and vegetables in his backyard. She feels his house is less alien with a growing garden. 'Do you want to see it, Tessa?'

'Yes, I'd like to see your garden.'

He surprises her by initiating a new topic. 'I enjoy driving in the countryside.'

'Do you?' Tessa feels talkative. There're some wonderful beaches and I like the bushwalks in the national parks. Once a snake slithered right in front of me on a track. Can you believe that? '

169

John Pappas is amused. 'Would you like a drive in the country? With your brother too,' he adds. Tessa isn't sure that she wants to drive with him in the country, but she's sure that she resents her brother acting as a chaperone. She doesn't answer.

'I'll ask your father.'

John Pappas is more communicative these days, but never talkative. Tessa finds him intelligent, but not, intellectual. The Saturday meetings don't seem as long.

A letter arrives from David.

Dear Tessa

I'm working very hard. The seasons. change here so dramatically, unlike home. Spring is everywhere and there are robins and sparrows and the English birds that the great poets write about. I still miss the kookaburras with their cackling laugh and appalling antics. They'd steal everybody's lunch.

I love reading the poetry you send me about the inner city with purple lilacs hanging from decaying balconies. I imagine the narrow stair- cases you write about, creaking up towards a garret where we can meet. You need to write about a marble fireplace in one special terrace, where we can lie casually on soft Persian carpets writing our great works.

I like you being a poet. I think about you often, especially late at night when I'm looking out of the window of my room onto Cambridge's cloisters.

I've been working such long hours that I'm exhausted. I'm finding myself obsessive, unable to drag myself away from the books. Sydney will be good for me. I'm trying to get away earlier, maybe even October. That's only four months away.

I want to meet your Athena. I expect you to show everyone how clever you are in your exams.

Love David

Tessa avoids her father, but he catches her on the stairs going up to her room.' Tessa, how do you like John Pappas and Paul Couris?'

Tessa stammers. 'I don't know them yet.'

'How long will it take to know them?' Her father demands.

She doesn't answer.

***

John Pappas arrives to take Tessa and her brother on the drive into the countryside. Mrs Kassis fusses, bringing coffee and biscuits. Mr Kassis asks where he is going. 'I've booked a special restaurant overlooking the Megalong Valley for our lunch.'

Mr Kassis approves.

'That'll be nice.' Tessa's surprised that she means it. They get up to leave. Peter runs upstairs because he's forgotten his jumper and it's cold in the mountains in winter.

As Tessa gets into the car, John Pappas says something strange. 'I am a plain man, Tessa. I am educated, although not as educated as you, but I am honest and hard working. I will look after you.'

Peter races out of the house and sprints to the car. 'Let's go. Where are we going, by the way?'

'The Blue Mountains.' John Pappas starts the car. The white ghost gums should look beautiful now.'

Tessa forces her father's plans out of her thoughts. *I'm going to have a good time.* 'Can I play my Elvis tape?'

John Pappas nods. Peter moans. Tessa inserts the tape into the car's cassette deck. She hums to the songs, while they pass the shops and caryards and head into the suburbs with their red brick cottages, and European trees. The blue bush of the Great Dividing Range rises on the horizon. They begin to climb through forests of mountain gums, with grey- brown bark' exposing creamy branches. Red and blue rosellas flash colour between the blue-green and white.

The Hydro Majestic Hotel with its imposing round dome and spreading annexes looks out of place in the mountains. Like a European spa house, it's strangely out-of-place, looking out over native scrub and trees. John Pappas parks against its heavy sandstone gate.

Jumping out of the car, Tessa leads the men into the expansive lounge with its large, fireplace. Worn leather armchairs and floral carpet show modern neglect and past comfort. Tessa runs her hand over the leather. Wide windows look out over the Megalong Valley in a panorama of dissipating mist and treetops. Tessa points at the red and blue rosellas flashing between branches. She turns to John Pappas. 'I love this.' He nods.

Peter and John Pappas discuss cars, while roast chicken, baked potatoes and peas are served. Tessa's excitement at the arrival of chocolate pudding covered in custard makes John Pappas smile. 'You enjoy chocolate?' Tessa nods as she licks the large spoon. 'Are you enjoying this trip into the mountains, Tessa?'

'I really like it.'

John Pappas determinedly steers the conversation away from cars. They talk about the native birds and animals that inhabit the view through the large glass windows. 'Can we walk into the valley after lunch?'

'Yes.' John Pappas agrees.

They wander down the yellow dirt track, stopping by a creek to watch the water bubble over rocks. Tessa flicks water at Peter, who flicks it back and they end up chasing each other through the bush. John Pappas smiles.

When they return home, they 're tired, but happy. Tessa races to her room to avoid her father.

***

The coming of the mid-year exams gives Tessa relief from the ritual courting patterns of Paul Couris and John Pappas. Her father accepts her excuses that she has to study and has no time for them. She is free for a month. No family, no John Pappas, no Paul Couris. Nothing except Athena and Jenny and Shakespeare, Wordsworth, T. S. Eliot's Prufrock.

The month ends. The exams are over and so is the moratorium. It marks the beginning of a campaign which is relentless. Mr Kassis stalks his daughter, cornering her, releasing her, cornering her. Tessa tries to escape into her poetry, study, cooking with her mother, but Mr Kassis pursues her. He tracks her in the kitchen, out into the garden, up the stairs to her room. She hides in her room, or flees to university and her creative writing group. She retreats into conferences with Athena and Jenny.

'Just tell your father you're not ready to get married.'

'I feel too exhausted. I just can't face the confrontation.' *Am I Prufrock? Do I dare? Do I dare?*

173

Tessa panics, drowning like Prufrock as John Pappas and Paul Couris and his mother visit again and again.

Tessa has less excuses to delay the decision and her father's demands. She asks her brother to help stop the pursuit.

'I can't do anything, Tessa.'

Her father traps her between the kitchen and the back door. 'What have you decided?'

'Give me till Christmas, Papa. Christmas,' Tessa whispers, scurrying to her room.

Chapter 21

Tessa shields herself from Mr Kassis by focusing on university studies. She talks at Jenny about the characters, their relationships and obsessions until Jenny refuses to listen anymore. 'Give me a break, Tessa. Remember my favourite subject is math, not literature.'

'And James.' Tessa's sharp. 'You talk about him all the time.'

'He's real at least.' Jenny blushes. She has filled the prescription the family planning doctor gave her.

'Sorry, Jenny. There's just a lot of pressure on.'

They descend the stairs into The Pit. 'Did you hear? The first test-tube baby,' Athena calls out to them as they walk in. She's already writing an article.

'Not very romantic.' Jenny throws her bag down on a chair.

Handing Tessa a newspaper clipping, Athena types the headline. LOUISE BROWN BORN FROM A TEST TUBE.

Tessa looks at the newspaper photo of the baby girl clenching her fists. 'It's amazing.' She rests her finger on the picture. 'Does it make scientists God?'

'I don't know, Tessa.' Athena bangs away at the keys. 'But it's powerful. A woman can have a baby without sex, without a man.'

Tessa looks over at Jenny flirting with Joel. 'A test tube seems so cold.'

'Yes, but Louise Brown wouldn't be here without it.'

'It bypasses men, doesn't it?' She puts down the newspaper. 'Where does that leave love?'

'Louise Brown's mother loves her baby, I'm sure.' Athena stops typing. 'I don't understand men and love, Tessa. Well, not after Christos.' Athena presses her fingers against. her lips. 'It's like we're on different wavelengths. They have sex and we make love.'

'I don't think that's all of it, Athena.'

'Maybe not, but it's part of it.' Athena looks up at Jenny who's brought over coffee for them. 'I'd like to have a baby one day with the man I love and who loves me.'

'Wouldn't we all.' Jenny agrees.

That afternoon, after classes, after getting home to her mother and biscuits, Tessa takes her rug and her D. H. Lawrence novel to the park. The winter leaves are golden, carpeting the pathways with crackles and rustles as she wanders to the sandstone memorial. White cockatoos are perched there until she disturbs them and. they flap away. Tessa wraps the blanket around her. Leaning against the sandstone, she closes her eyes, enjoying the paradox of winter sun and cold wind. She drifts into the gamekeeper's arms as he explores Lady Chatterley's 'warm, soft body', kissing her navel, revelling in the 'pure peace' of entering 'into the body of the woman'. Tessa runs her hands down her sides, sensing the glide of his cheek on her thighs and belly and buttocks, and the close brushing of his moustache and his soft thick hair'. *Is it the gamekeeper? Heathcliff? David?* She opens her eyes to see John Pappas and test-tube passion.

That evening, Mr Kassis shakes his head at 'unnatural' babies. 'What is happening in this world?' He waits for Tessa's comments, but she makes none as she arranges the pink winter roses in an alabaster vase. 'Tessa have you something to say?'

She does not look up as she bends to smell the sweet scent. 'No, Papa. I haven't thought about it.'

There has been a silence between them since that day he struck her. Tessa has retreated further into the garden. When John Pappas visits, he enjoys working with her, cutting back the branches, turning the soil, helping the winter roses thrive. Her mother approves as Tessa hides herself between weeds and butterflies. There's a letter from David. He's really coming back. Only two and a half months to wait. Tessa puts the letter in her pocket. She can hardly concentrate on her mother's endless questions about Sunday lunch for Paul Couris and his mother and how fresh the bread is from the local bakery and the excitement of a baby for a cousin. 'I have knitted two pairs of white booties and a bonnet with satin ribbons.'

Tessa pretends to answer. 'Yes, yes, yes!' *I don't care, don't you understand, Mother? In two months, I'll see David and he'll love me like the gamekeeper because I'm Lady Chatterley. Can't you see?*

'And we will go next Saturday afternoon to your cousins for the party for the baby that will come soon.'

***

The Kassis family has been invited for dinner to the Pappas house. Peter and Tessa race each other down the staircase, making Mr Kassis laugh. 'You behave yourself, children.' Mrs Kassis carries the sweet baklava she's baked for the occasion and the sugared almonds she's specially wrapped in embroidered cloth. Mr Kassis takes two bottles of ouzo.

As he drives up the circular driveway to the Pappas house, he approves of the wide driveway. 'Tessa, it is enough for four cars. Tessa ignores her father's admiration for the large pebble entrance.

Mr Pappas greets Mr Kassis with open arms. The two fathers hug each other, then exchange pleasure in the giving and receiving of Mr Kassis' gifts.

After the greetings and the ritual compliments on each other's appearance and the house, the men go to the lounge room. Mr Pappas opens the bottle of ouzo and pours a glass for Peter and Mr Kassis, then himself and John Pappas. 'Strong.' Mr Pappas approves and smiles. Tessa and Mrs Kassis are already in the kitchen helping Mrs Pappas with the meal.

The house, with its modern furniture and leather armchairs, is different to the Kassis '. Only an icon in the corner links the two homes. The kitchen is smart, with black marble benches and oak-crafted cupboards. The dishwasher whirrs as they arrange the salads. Mrs Kassis shakes her head. 'I could never use a dishwasher.' She likes immersing her hands in sudsy water, wiping the oil from white china so that it sparkles, smelling of lemon. No, she does not want a dishwasher.

The table is laid with silver service. The centre-piece is a painted glass bowl overflowing with out- of-season peaches, plums, cantaloupe and strawberries. The meal is generous, overflowing like the fruits in the bowl. Moussaka is layered heavily with black eggplant and the leanest cut of topside mince. Salads of red tomatoes from the garden and black olives and white feta spill over the edges of bowls. The bread is fresh, bought from the bakery because the parents only eat freshly baked bread, like it was at their Greek village.

White and red Australian wines are poured generously. The Pappas' went to the Hunter Valley once and saw the vines. carrying heavy purple and yellow grapes. They saw the rich soil and they believe Australian wine is the best. 'Good wine,' Mr Kassis says, which makes Mr Pappas smile. Tessa is startled by memories of the Geography excursion and the afternoons of red wine and David in the university rooms. She looks at John Pappas, who sits comfortably in his home. He is handsome, she thinks.

The men wipe their mouths with large cloth napkins, burping behind the folds. They complement Mrs Pappas on her moussaka and her tense face relaxes into satisfaction. They enjoy the ripe fruit brought from up North, where the sun is hot.

Coffee is served in the lounge room., Once everyone settles, Mrs Pappas joins them, sitting between Tessa and her mother. She commences a monologue on the success of the church fete and how much money has been raised for the Greek school. Tessa's mother listens keenly, while Tessa pretends to be interested. She looks out of the window into the garden.

The men talk business. The old Mr Pappas is well-off. He owns four houses that he rents. Tessa catches some of the conversation about tenants and taxes and blocking a window in a side wall. George Pappas is seventy-four years old. He still looks young to Tessa. John Pappas's father is strong, like the son.

George Pappas started his life in Australia as a young man in a factory and he worked hard, like Mr Kassis. His children make him proud. His daughter has three children already. His son John Pappas has never disappointed him and now is ready to marry.

George Pappas looks at Tessa. A good choice, with her bright eyes and intelligence. For a moment he frowns. He notices her distance from the older women. Her aspirations seem different to theirs and to his son's. He shakes his head. No, she will be a good wife.

John Pappas leaves his father and Mr Kassis to sit beside Tessa.

Chapter 22

Tessa and Mrs Kassis arrive with the knitted bonnet and booties for their cousin's coming baby. Their cousin's mother greets them. Already, a large crowd of women have arrived at the baby shower. Tessa kisses her cousin, remembering her as a girl playing in the church courtyard. She's twenty-one now and her stomach bulges under her loose dress. Tessa unconsciously rubs her hands over her flat stomach. Athena is inside with her mother. She waves at Tessa to come over. There are drinks and cakes and gifts of nappies, bibs, rugs and rattles and women discussing wind and burping. Everyone praises Mrs Kassis's knitting. Mrs Kassis glows with the praise, and she turns to Athena's mother who is now sitting beside her. Tessa will be married soon and there will be babies.'

Tessa grimaces at her mother, who is speaking so loudly everyone can hear. Athena nudges Tessa. 'I gave her that rug.' The cousin is holding a baby rug to the light so that the embroidered rabbit's ears look like they are wiggling. There's laughing, and Tessa's cousin runs to the bathroom. There's more laughing because they all know about the baby pressing on her bladder.

Tessa lies back against the lounge watching her cousin returning from the bathroom, slowed by her protruding stomach. The laughter of the women rises into a crescendo, making Tessa's head whirl like dancing at the Young Greek Matron's Ball. She presses Athena's arm. 'I can't wait to get away from this.

'Tessa, your cousin's happy.'

'I suppose so.' She changes the subject. 'Won't our holiday to the Greek Islands be special?'

Athena looks over to her mother, who is still sitting next to Mrs Kassis. 'Let's not talk about it here. My parents are still pretty upset about me going.'

Tessa nods. They spend the rest of the afternoon watching baby presents being opened and eating sweet cakes.

That evening Mr Kassis strides into his house. He calls for Tessa. Mrs Kassis looks into the corridor. 'Tessa, come out of the kitchen, I have something for you.'

'What is it, Father?' Tessa follows him into the sitting room.

'Sit down, Tessa. I have spoken to my brother.' He rubs his hand along his chin. 'I have not seen him since he was a child. I was glad to talk to him.' He pulls an envelope out of the inside pocket of his jacket. 'This is for you.' She looks curiously at her father. 'Open it.'

Mrs Kassis watches from the doorway as Tessa pulls out the plane ticket to Greece. 'Papa.' She goes to Mr Kassis and puts her arms around him. 'Thank you so much.'

He smiles. 'My brother and his wife are looking forward to you staying with them. I hope it will be a good journey for you. You will learn about your family.'

'I can't believe I'm really going.'

'I keep my word and it is a good thing before you marry.' He reaches for his pipe. 'You do like John Pappas?'

She holds the ticket tightly. 'Yes.'

Mr Kassis lights his pipe. Mrs Kassis joins them with coffee and almond biscuits. Tessa pours coffee for her father. 'Thank you, Tessa.' He watches her noiselessly arrange the cups and saucers. Her black hair sways with her movements as she bends. He reaches for her arm. 'Tessa, you are a good daughter. Please. Sit down, I would like to talk.' He waits for her to settle and for his thoughts to collect.

'You know when you were born, the doctor came and told me that you were a girl. I did not want a girl. My first born was to be a boy.' He draws smoke from his pipe. 'I was angry at your mother.' He looks at Mrs Kassis, who laughs softly. 'I should not have been. She was tired. Your mother wrapped you in a soft blanket that she had knitted. I looked inside that blanket and I saw a small fierce baby with black hair and hands locked into two tight fists. I put a finger into each of your fists and you grabbed them. You lifted your head to look at me and the doctor said that you were strong. Other babies did not lift their heads to stare at their fathers.' He puts down his pipe. 'I was glad then that you were a girl.'

Tessa rubs her eyes. 'And I'm glad you're my father.'

'You understand me always. I knew you saw the Mediterranean Sea I swam in as a boy. You knew the pain of my calloused hands when I drew fishing nets into the boat with my father. You understood how hard it was when I left my homeland for this strange country.'

Tessa gets up from the lounge and goes to her father. She kisses him. 'Thank you.'

***

When Athena, Jenny and Tessa meet, they shout excitedly at each other. 'I've got the tickets,' Tessa is

183

breathless. Jenny jumps up and down, making her blonde hair bob. It tips her shoulders these days. 'You should see how jealous James is. He doesn't think it's such a great idea that I go now.'

'But you are coming with us?' Tessa points to her ticket.

'Yes, yes, after all the waitressing I've done, I deserve a holiday. All I've got to do is pass my exams. I won't be going if I have to re-sit them in the holidays.'

'That won't happen. I'll help you, Jenny.' Tessa bites her nails. 'Maybe I can get even more help for you.'

'Stop biting your nails. How?'

Tessa puts her hands behind her back. 'I got a phone call. He's coming for a visit. Professor Davids. He'll be here tomorrow.'

Athena and Jenny splutter questions. 'Where? How long? How come? Where are you meeting?'

Tessa throws her bag over her shoulder and starts walking towards the library. 'Do I look like his personal assistant? How would I know?'

'Come on, tell us.' Jenny and Athena tag behind her, bothering her until she answers.

'Tomorrow. I'm meeting him here tomorrow.'

***

The night is restless, with the trees tapping at her window. She closes it tightly, shutting out her father. She has other dreams tonight. David.

It's the morning and Tessa gulps down an orange juice, avoiding her mother and the dishes. 'Sorry, I have to be at uni early today.' Peter isn't interested as he taps the top of his boiled egg.

184

Mr Kassis puts down his cup. 'Then you had better go, Tessa.'

David. Tessa runs down the street, panting as she boards the bus, but the bus is slow. Peak hour traffic makes it crawl through the suburbs until Tessa is biting her nails and kicking the seat in front. She practises how she's going to act when she meets him. Calm. *I'll just stand there looking sophisticated. He hardly wrote to me, and I waited and waited for his letters, but he said he was busy... and I can't believe it. He's here.* The bus stops. Tessa races past the library and the students loitering. She's standing on the front lawn. He's not there. Looking down at her sandalled feet, she concentrates on the green shoots of the grass.

Arms engulf her. He's warm and tender and she leans against him. 'Tessa, I missed you.'

Liar. But I don't care. Liar.

Stroking her face, he asks. 'Did you miss me?' She doesn't answer as he leads her towards the Moreton Bay fig with its thick heavy roots spreading into the grass. They sit down leaning against the roots.

She touches his black moustache. 'Yes.'

He asks her about her studies. She answers in monosyllables, until he stops asking. 'Can I tell you about Cambridge?' Tessa nods. He talks about the colleges where students still eat together in the great hall overseen by professors and teachers, and how he tutored them under the stone arches that reminded him of his university at home. They smile at the stodgy professors who carefully hide behind 'proper' accents and British reserve. Her nervousness eases as his words spread between the branches of the Moreton Bay fig and her thoughts. He kisses each of her fingers. 'Can you talk now?'

Nodding, she whispers, 'It's hard.' She bites her fingernails making him laugh. He takes her hands.

Tessa starts, slowly at first, talking in fragments about her studies, Athena, Jenny, Christmas in the Greek Islands, jumbling John Pappas and her father and Paul Couris into a lolly jar of disconnected patterns until David shakes his head. 'Slower, Tessa. Slower.'

Distracted, unsure of what she's said or is saying, she murmurs 'Sorry.'

David kisses her lips, stopping the 'sorry' and the jumble. 'The Greek Islands?'

'My father is letting me visit the islands with Athena and Jenny.' She talks about the ancient temples and white sands until she suddenly closes her eyes tight. She leans against his shoulder.

'What's wrong?'

Opening her eyes, she stares into his face. 'Your eyes look like the Mediterranean Sea. Really blue.'

'Tessa, have you heard of evasion?'

'I want to tell you...' She takes a deep breath. 'I'm selfish, you know. My parents have given me everything and they've really struggled. I've never struggled. I want to be a good daughter because I love them and it's right, but,' whispering, 'I don't think I can be.' She waits. 'And there's John Pappas.'

'Who's he?'

'My parents like him. His father worked really hard. I don't like his mother.' Her words jerk against each other. 'He grows oranges in his garden. He drives into the bush. I like that.'

'What are you talking about, Tessa?'

John Pappas.' She presses David's hand. 'He's big.'
Tessa surprises herself. 'I'm frightened of him.' She
hadn't known she was frightened of him. 'My father has
chosen him as my husband. Or I can have Paul Couris
who, is smaller but has a mother who sits disapproving
of me.' Her words tumble out of the lolly jar. 'She wears
black and would live with me supervising the house,
making sure I'm a proper wife. My 'father wants me to
choose, so he can have grandchildren, so that I can be
moulded into my mother. A bent, tortured mould, like
the Chinese women who had their feet bound in cloth.
They couldn't run, just hobble and they could never
take the bandages off their feet because the pain would
kill them and he says I have to and I love my father and I
can't...'

David holds Tessa until her words stop, until she's
breathless, until she's protected by his arms.

Chapter 23

Jenny shakes her paint brush at Tessa. 'Can you believe that this is the last room. No more painting needed at this refuge. Well, at least for now.'

James throws down his brush. 'That's it. I need a beer. So, who's your friend Tessa?'

'David.'

Jenny puts down her brush too. She hadn't noticed him in the room before. For a moment she's uncomfortable, remembering him as the arrogant professor at her first lectures. She refuses to be intimidated and puts out her paint-splattered hand.

James hands him a beer. 'What can you do, with women? I'm supposed to be finishing my physics lab now, but look at me.' Two small boys race past, one sticking out his hand to run his finger along the wet paint. 'Hey, don't touch, ' James shouts as they disappear down the corridor.

'So, can you take a break? It's lunchtime and I sort of insisted that David come down here to meet you. Athena will be here soon as well.'

'We're finished, aren't we James?' Jenny pulls his shirt. 'And James is always starving.'

'I'm a growing boy.' He laughs. 'And a man needs to keep up his strength.'

Jenny rolls her eyes and pats his stomach.

As they strip off their painting gear, Jenny talks about the refuge. 'There are some pretty awful stories. The refuge is the only safe house these women and kids have.' Jenny looks over at Tessa. 'Even if painting is the only thing we do, it's helping.'

'You've done a few other things too, like shouting at women's rallies and knocking everyone over with your banners.'

'I only knocked over a few undesirables,' Jenny jokes. 'You know James and Tessa have become excellent painters since the refuge.'

Athena breezes into the house. A few women say hello as she hands a little girl a fluffy green dog. 'I didn't forget.' The girl scurries off to a corner with the toy.

'Where are you?' Her voice rings through the passageway. 'Everything looks great.' She bumps into them, coming out of the newly painted room.

'Athena, this is my friend David.'

'Great to meet you David.' Tessa's talked a lot about you.' Smiling, he shakes her hand. 'David, now that you're back in Australia, Tessa and I have made serious plans.' He looks curious. 'Don't worry. It's only the Australian initiation ceremony. Lunch with pies, peas and mash.' Everyone laughs as Athena leads them to the local hotel.

'I've missed a good meat pie and a cold beer. I couldn't get used to warm ale and cold pork pies in England.'

'That sounds pretty rough to me,' James agrees. Nudging Tessa, Athena whispers,

'Heathcliff. Definitely, Heathcliff.'

'Don't,' Tessa nudges her back.

It's one of those afternoons that Tessa never imagined she'd be part of. Real friends, coffee, conversation about literature and Cambridge, about women's rights and their futures. James wants to be a physicist.

'There are no jobs. Have you considered teaching physics?' David bites into his pie. 'Unemployment for new graduates is a real problem but there are opportunities in teaching.'

'Look, they've got lamingtons.' Athena points to the chocolate and coconut covered sponges under the glass dome on the counter. 'You have to have one of them. It'll make it a real coming home.'

'Lamingtons. I haven't had them for a long time.' While James and David eat lamingtons, Tessa and Jenny and Athena congregate in the Ladies. 'He's cute,' Jenny says.

'I remember when you didn't think he was.' Tessa smiles.

'Mistake. I think my judgment was affected by the rotten marks he gave me. He's definitely cute.'

Athena holds her hand. 'Do you love him?'

Tessa nods. 'Yes. Yes.'

They leave the hotel to go in their different directions. Tessa and David wander to the terrace where David is staying. The terrace is old and peeling, with white jasmine growing between the spears of the wrought-iron fence. 'This is romantic, David.'

The stairway inside is steep and Tessa trips as she climbs it. David catches her. They drink wine on the balcony. David still enjoys the reds, but Tessa wrinkles her nose.

'It takes time to enjoy red wine. Obviously, your university days haven't been very wild, otherwise you'd be used to it by now.'

She sips a little more from her glass. 'Horrible.'

He smiles.

'Did you like my friends, David?'

'Yes.' He finishes his glass of wine. He takes her hands and leads her to the sofa in the lounge room.

'Now, Tessa let's talk about John Pappas, or is it Paul Couris?'

John Pappas,' she whispers. 'What do you want?'

'I don't want to be married. And not to John Pappas. My father...' She rubs the back of her hand. 'I have to give him an answer before Christmas.'

'Can I speak to your father?'

'I don't know. I'm scared.' She looks up at him. 'Yes.'.

***

David is invited for dinner. He arrives at eight in the evening. Mr Kassis is honoured that Tessa's old professor is dining at his house.

The sitting room is more formal than usual for this important guest, with the best silver displayed and the newspapers neatly folded into racks. Mr Kassis welcomes the professor, while Mrs Kassis disappears into the kitchen with Tessa. The conversation between the men slips in and around books and Cambridge and Tessa's abilities. Peter discusses his law degree. 'You'll get a good job with that degree.' Mr Kassis approves the professor's opinion.

There are white bone china plates and crystal glasses and silver cutlery. Tessa carries out the dolmades. She brushes David 's arm as he discusses with Mr Kassis opportunities for Peter after he finishes law. She leans against David, forking curled calamari onto his plate.

Only after the main meal, when they are sitting in comfortable lounge chairs, when the good food makes Mr Kassis mellow and the women are serving coffee and cakes and ouzo, does the conversation change.

'Tessa's very gifted. I hope she will go on to further studies.'

'Thank you. Tessa is clever, but Tessa has other plans.' Mr Kassis offers David almond biscuits. 'Please, take some. They are very good.' David puts a biscuit on his plate.

'I am sure you appreciate the importance of learning, Mr Kassis.'

'Yes, that is why she is at the university.'

'She's only starting. There's a long way to go before she finishes university.'

'That is for me to decide, Professor Davids.'

'Surely she has a choice in it.'

Mr Kassis stiffens. 'My daughter has choices.'

'Then will you allow her to choose to continue her studies or not?'

Tessa interrupts, 'I'd like to do honours.'

'I do not wish to discuss this now with Professor Davids.'

'But he's my old professor.'

'And I am your father.'

Peter tries to distract Mr Kassis. 'Would anyone like some more ouzo?'

'No.' His father's voice bristles.

'It would be a shame for Tessa not to go on.'

'Are you' interfering in my family?'

'I just want to bring to your attention Tessa's talent.'

'I do not need you to do that. I know my daughter.'

Mr Kassis demands, 'Why are you here? To tell me how to look after my daughter?'

'I just want the best for Tessa.'

'I know what is the best for my daughter.'

'You want Tessa to be happy?'

Mr Kassis stands. 'Happy? What do you know about happy and my daughter?'

David stands up, looking at Tessa. She's watching him. He turns to the father. 'I care for Tessa as a teacher.'

'Do you think that matters?'

David waits. 'And as a man.' He's surprised at what he's saying.

The father is rigid. 'What gives you the right to insult me?'

'It's not meant as an insult.'

'She is to be married to John Pappas. You will leave my house now.'

Tessa stands up. 'No, Papa.'

Mr Kassis strides towards her and puts his hands on her shoulders, pushing her back down onto the floral settee.

'Stop it, Sir.'

'I have told you to leave, Professor Davids.'

He takes Tessa's hand. 'Tessa, I want you to come with me. Will you?'

Mr Kassis slams his arm between their hands. 'You go now!' He raises his fists, threatening to hit David.

'No.' Mrs Kassis calls out to her husband.

'Tessa, go to your room.'

She stands still.

'Tessa come with me.'

He spits at David. 'Have you seduced my daughter?'

'No, Sir.'

'Get out. Get out.' He moves closer to David, shoving his hand against David's chest. 'Get out.'

'Not until you hear me.'

'Hear you? There is nothing you can say. You are a stranger who has intruded on my daughter and her family. I will throw you out if you do not leave.'

'Your daughter has done nothing wrong.'

Tessa grabs David's arm.

'Go to your room, Tessa.'

She holds onto David tighter.

Mr Kassis' hands shove harder, pushing David towards the front door, pushing until he's pressing his back against the doorknob. 'Leave. Leave. Leave.' The doorknob juts into David's spine.

Mr Kassis shoves his daughter away so that she falls to the floor. David bends to help her up. Mr Kassis slams his fist into David's stomach, winding him, slamming his fist again into him, again into him, slamming open the door, forcing him through it, shoving him outside into the night.

Chapter 24

Tessa's curled on her bed when her brother comes into her room.

'Are you awake?' Muffled sounds come from under the doona. 'It's me.'

Tessa pushes the doona down.

'You've been crying.' He sits on her bed. 'I've never seen him like that.'

Tessa whispers, 'He's hit me before. No one's allowed to think for themselves.'

'He's the father. But I didn't think he'd do that.'

'He's a dictator, Peter. Mama is so weak, it's worse. I can't bear it. I can't.' She shivers. 'What about David? Do you think he's all right?'

'I don't know. I'd say it's bad.'

'He didn't hit him back. I respect David for that.'

Peter shakes his head. 'I'd have hit him.'

'I've got to find out how David is. If I phone him, will you watch out?'

'Suppose so. Just let me check that the parents aren't around. Keep it short.'

Tessa struggles out of bed. She stands close to her brother. 'This is the first time you've gone against him.'

'It was wrong.' He looks down the corridor. 'But hurry up, there's been enough trouble tonight.'

She puts her hand on his shoulder. 'This means a lot to me.'

Tessa pads to the corridor phone. The phone rings and rings. Peter paces. Eventually, there's an answer. 'Is that you, David?' There's silence. 'Are you all right?'

'Tessa?' His voice is shaky. 'Are you all right?'

195

'I'm okay. I'm going back to England in a few days.' David speaks carefully. 'Come with me.'

She doesn't speak for a moment. 'David, I want to.' She holds the phone close to her. 'It's beautiful that you have asked me, but I can't. Not like this.'

'I'm worried. You'll be forced into something you don't want. Your father's lost control of himself. Will I try to talk to him again?'

Tessa stops him. 'Please, David. I don't want you to do anymore. I have to work it out myself.'

'You won't be able to.'

'Trust me, David'

'All right, but when will I see you?'

'I don't know. I'm a prisoner for a while, but it won' t be forever.'

Peter pulls at her sleeve. 'Hurry up.'

'I have to go.' She looks down the corridor. 'I'll make Papa keep his word. I'll be in Greece at Christmas and then I promise, I'll meet you. I promise.'

Peter whispers. 'Get off the phone. I think I hear someone coming.'

'I love you David. You were so brave to stand up to my father.'

Tessa, I love you too.'

***

Tessa doesn't see David before he flies back to England. She cries on the phone to Athena and Jenny. Alone in her room with her shells and icon and the trees banging against her window, she writes poetry for David.

Sunday mornings are for church. The afternoons are for her garden because Paul Couris and his mother don't visit anymore. John Pappas visits every Saturday. Tessa strips the green leaves off the carnations she's cut from the garden. She places the tall stalks in the crystal vase, before teasing the pink buds into lacey petals. She bends to smell the scents of the flowers, ignoring her father who passes by, as if they are strangers.

Tessa doesn't know that her father has made arrangements with George Pappas. She doesn't know there's been a settlement. Mr Kassis will pay for the wedding and a cottage on the coast for his daughter and John Pappas. 'An investment for the future,' he tells George Pappas, who nods approvingly. Tessa doesn't know she's engaged to be married.

It's a relief to leave for university each morning, even though she has a curfew these days. There's only a week left before exams and then the Christmas vacation. Her mother stands at the door. There is a special dinner tonight. 'Our priest and the Pappas' are here for dinner.' She whispers. 'For the announcement. Your father will...'

Tessa only half listens. She does not look at her mother who didn't defend her, who is lonely and waits for her. Her mother's betrayal makes Tessa unable to hug or touch her or hum Greek songs with her in the kitchen. *You didn't protect me. You should have protected me.*

Athena and Jenny are waiting for Tessa in the cafeteria. They have the Greek newspaper in front of them. 'Can you read Greek now, Jenny?' Tessa sits down.

'Did you know about this?' Athena points to the paper.

Tessa leans over, reading the four lines boxed in by a heavy black border. Suddenly she can't breathe. Gasping for air, the lines blur. Then clear. She reads the announcement. Tessa Kassis and John Pappas. Engaged to John Pappas. 'It can't be true. Papa can't …'

Athena squeezes her hand. 'I'm so sorry. So Sorry.'

Jenny puts her arms around Tessa.

Tessa begins to breathe again. 'I'm not marrying anyone. He can't make me. I won't do it.'

Athena smooths the crushed newspaper. 'Arranged marriages. Family introductions. They happen. Lebanese, Turkish, Chinese, Indian … not only Greeks.'

'Well, don't marry him, if you don't want to.'

'Jenny, it's not so easy.' Athena looks at Tessa. 'We love our community. Our family. If Tessa doesn't do what her father says, she could lose her family and everyone. Be disinherited, have no way to support herself. I don't know.'

Tessa folds the newspaper and puts it in her bag. 'I'm not married yet and I am going to the Greek Islands.'

Athena grabs her arm. 'Don't make a scene with your father. It'll be worse. Persuade him. Be clever, Tessa. Do you want me to come with you?'

'No. I have to do this myself. Whatever happens.'

When Tessa arrives home that afternoon, her father is waiting for her. She follows him into the sitting room, past the dining table which is already set with the Kassis' best dishes and a central floral arrangement with orange birds of paradise.

He sits down in his armchair. 'I have chosen to forget what you have done. The professor is gone now.'

Tessa bites her lip. *Forget. I can't forget.*

'We have been honoured. The priest is coming for dinner to bless you and John Pappas.'

'John Pappas. Why?' *How could you? It's like I'm nothing.*

'You had enough time to choose, but you did not. I know what is best.'

Think Tessa. Think. Be like Athena. 'You want me to get a degree first, don't you Father?'

'Yes. Your degree first and then at the finish of next year, you will marry.' Mr Kassis talks about plans for her future. 'You do not need to work when you are married to John Pappas.' He reaches for his pipe. 'And the little house I have bought for you both, sits on a cliff overlooking the ocean. It will go up in value.' He sucks in the air from his pipe to make sure that it is unblocked. 'It is a special place, Tessa. We will drive together and see it.'

'And is the house like the houses in Greece?'

'Greece? No. This is an Australian house made with red brick and a roof of tiles. There is a large wooden veranda. You can sit out on the veranda and watch the sea. You will like that, Tessa.'

Let him talk. Let him talk. Tessa studies his strong fingers pushing the tobacco into the pipe. He lights his pipe, drawing the smoke in slowly. 'The houses on the Mediterranean in Greece are white with. flat roofs. I would like you to see it one day.'

She takes a breath. 'But I will, soon. When I go to Greece at Christmas'.'

'I do not know.' Mr Kassis takes out his pipe from his mouth. 'Greece.'

'You promised, Papa. I have the ticket.'

He stops to think. 'I promised. Then I must keep my promise.'

***

John Pappas stands behind his parents as they are greeted. He smiles at Tessa, but looks tired. He explains that he'll have to leave early because there's urgent work at the garage. 'I'm starting at five a.m. tomorrow. My best mechanic is sick and three cars were towed into the garage today.'

Mr Kassis approves John Pappas's work ethic. 'It is important then.'

John Pappas usually enjoys the wires and batteries, adjusting engines, tuning cars until they purr perfectly, but he has rushed his work today, tightening the nuts and bolts on the last car too quickly. It worries him. His mother motions to Tessa. 'You should make my son comfortable. Can't you see that he is tired? Get him some ouzo.'

Tessa bristles as she shows John Pappas the lounge, while his mother approves. Mrs Pappas admires her son. Even though others were more talented, he always worked hard. At football, he would kick the ball, running single-mindedly towards the goal until he won. She knows Tessa isn't good enough for him.

The dinner goes smoothly as the women serve the priest and the men. The priest blesses the couple to the general approval of the parents before he leaves. Tessa reddens as John Pappas watches her.

Mr Kassis pours scotch for George Pappas and his son. 'Let us toast this engagement.' They raise their glasses and scoff it down. George Pappas announces, 'My son needs a real celebration. Next week, the men.

200

will celebrate.' The fathers settle down to talk about the boys' night out and business. John Pappas half listens to them, watching Tessa from the corner of his eye. When he sees her escape into the garden, he follows her.

She's standing in the flower bed between pink carnations and yellow daffodils. John Pappas startles her when his thick hands circle her waist from behind. 'Oh, it's you. You gave me a shock.' She tries to slip away, but his hands are strong from his work. She can't move.

'Do you like these flowers, Tessa?'

'Yes. I'll pick some for you, if you let me go.'

'No. It's all right.' He turns her around so that she faces him. Then he bends his head forward and places his lips over hers, sucking her tongue into his mouth until she wants to gag.

Chapter 25

Examinations start. Peter locks himself in his room to study, only emerging for food. 'I want to do more than pass,' he tells Tessa as he shuts the door on her.

'Have you heard of antisocial, Peter?'

A laugh comes through the keyhole. 'Go and study.'

Tessa has a final reprieve from John Pappas and his mother. *I think I hate Mrs Pappas.*

John Pappas's' night out with the men arrives. The party includes Mr Kassis, George Pappas, cousins, friends. The mechanics who work for John Pappas come too. His mechanics like him because he's a fair boss and works under the cars with them. They know he'll give them a big bonus at Christmas.

George Pappas chooses a strip club. His son agrees because he respects his father, but he doesn't understand why the strip club. He doesn't understand why his father sleeps with strange women. Women his mother suspects. It makes her dissatisfied, forcing her to turn to her son as if he's the answer to her unfulfilled marriage. His mother criticises Tessa.

'Stop. I don't want to hear any more about Tessa. She'll be my wife soon.' He walks out on his mother.

The men file down narrow steps, past glaring neon signs into a basement. There's loud music that makes them shout their orders for drinks that are too expensive. They take their drinks to tables and leer at women in gold G-strings. George Pappas slaps his son on the back. Mr Kassis looks at his watch. Jokes about marriage and getting caught. It make's some of the men laugh, or pretend to laugh. Breasts and bottoms exposed in beads hold John Pappas's interest briefly. He thinks of soft black hair and gentle lips.

Some of the men get drunk. John Pappas doesn't. John Pappas drinks whisky slowly, thinking to himself that life is working out as he planned. He has a good business, a large house and will marry Tessa. He used to notice Tessa as a young girl praying in the Greek Orthodox church. He'd watched her obey her parents and he'd waited for her to grow up.

Most of the men are drunk when they leave the strip club. John Pappas hails taxis for them.

At home, Tessa has a letter from David.

Darling Tessa

I'm working on my book. You're part of it and I can't wait to show you soon. You promised to meet me on one of those Greek Islands. I have already bought the ticket to Athens.

Late November winds gust across the commons preparing for Christmas here. I want to laugh at the cold that makes me shiver because I know that I'll soon be where there are gentler breezes with you.

Love David

The long university vacation begins. There's excitement as Jenny, Athena and Tessa make the final preparations for their holiday.

It's the day before Tessa goes. She persuades her mother to walk with her in the park. They wander towards the sandstone memorial and sit alongside it on the grass. 'Why don't you come with me to Greece, Mama?'

Mrs Kassis smiles. 'It is too late now. You are leaving tomorrow.'

'You could join me for just a few weeks.'

She shakes her head. 'Your father needs me here and who will look after Peter?'

'Peter? ' Tessa scoffs. 'He's not an excuse. Peter can find his own dirty socks under his bed and do his own laundry. Papa will be fine. It's just for a few weeks.'

Tessa watches her mother's movements. The touching of her wispy brown hair, the sweeping of imaginary dirt from her dress. 'I cannot go.'

'Please?'

She shakes her head. Mrs Kassis is a caged bird, her happiness dependent on the moods and activities of others. Sometimes her wings catch the wire. Now her door is open. She could be free, but she won't venture out of the wires. She doesn't need a prison.

She hesitates. 'Tessa, I know it has been hard on you, but it is for the best.'

'Yes, things turn out for the best.' Tessa hugs her. 'I'll miss you.'

Mrs Kassis smiles. 'Four weeks is a long time, but you will be back.' She stands up. 'John Pappas is coming for dinner. We have to go back.' Strolling between the trees and the lakes of the park, they pass black swans diving for bread thrown by children.

Dinner is pleasant, with Mr Kassis at the head of the table. John Pappas asks Tessa, 'Would you like to go for a walk outside?'

She doesn't want to, but her father answers for her. 'Go with him, Tessa. It is pleasant outside tonight.'

They head out into the darkness. John Pappas forages in his pocket. 'This is for you. Open it.' Tessa takes the package. The diamond ring is large, sparkling in the moonlight. 'Put it on.' She slips the ring onto her finger. He takes her in his arms. With his left hand, he rummages under her bra and squeezes her breast.

John Pappas leaves. Together, Tessa and Mrs Kassis clear the table, wash the dishes, restore the order of the house.

As Tessa says goodnight, her mother takes her hand, stroking it gently. 'I am glad you are going on this trip. I will miss you, but I am glad.'

Tessa wanders around her room, touching her shells, rustling through her writing, holding her golden icon, watching the bats soar into her park. She lies on her bed, with the icon still in her hand. Peter's classical music drifts into her room and she hears her father bang the front door, locking it carefully. To keep them all safe.

I'm afraid. Afraid. John Pappas. Can I really marry him? She presses her breasts, feeling his thick fingers burrowing into her. Turning into her pillow, she breathes the fresh starch of linen her mother's careful washing. *Can I leave you and Papa and Peter? It'd hurt you and... me.* The gold of the icon reflects the lights of the night and she rests it on her pillow. *Can I be good like I, when I was a little girl at church?* Dozing to dreams of candles and incense, she imagines Athena stroking her. David holding her. Tessa slips on a red dress. Mrs Kassis smiles. 'You look beautiful.'

Breakfast is different. Tessa doesn't serve today. 'Just sit and be with us,' her mother says.

Mr Kassis watches Tessa worry her cup. He takes her hand. 'I will miss you Tessa.'

Mrs Kassis catches her breath. 'I will too.'

'Just have a good holiday, Tessa.' Peter jumps up from the table. 'Come on Tessa. We've got to go. Don't want to be late for the plane.'

'No. You cannot be late.' Mr Kassis pushes his coffee cup aside.

The airport is crowded. Jenny's parents introduce themselves to Athena's and Tessa's parents. The Pappas' are there. James and Jenny are holding hands. Athena is in conference with her parents, who are warning her about Christos.

Mr Kassis hands Tessa travellers' cheques and money. 'You be careful.' His arms surround her, hugging her for a long time.

Mrs Kassis hovers, brushing Tessa's jacket, fiddling with the label on her bag, giving her almond biscuits wrapped in cloth for the flight. 'Mama, please. I don't want the biscuits.' Her mother's eyes cloud. 'No, no, I didn't mean that. I love the biscuits.'

'Mama, give her a break.' Peter gives Tessa a quick kiss.

Then there is John Pappas. He takes her hand, rolling the ring he gave her between his thumb and forefinger.

There are hugs and kisses and crying as the three young women walk towards the customs barriers. Tessa turns back for a moment to see her father watching her, as she leaves him. Mrs Kassis is crying. John Pappas looks handsome standing there, sure of his future.

Passports are shown. They board the plane. Settling into their seats, they look out over the tarmac. Seat belts are locked, safety instructions given and the plane starts moving, faster and faster until they're no longer in the air.

Jenny shows them a small sapphire ring with chips of diamonds surrounding it. 'It's from James.'

'Is that what you really want?' Tessa asks. 'And a baby one day.' It seems so long ago when they walked along that liquidambar lined street.

Tessa looks out of the window, watching the clouds divide her from home, her parents, John Pappas, twenty years in her father's house. *Mama, I love you Papa. I love you.*

She circles the ring, slipping, sliding it along her finger as David's recitation of the woman wailing for her 'demon lover' plays tricks of memory. *David, you'll be waiting for me in Greece.*

Suddenly she shudders. John Pappas is in the garden sucking at her mouth, with her father approving, her mother layering the honey pastry of baklava, the priest blessing her swelling stomach. *NO. NO.* Jolting forward, the seat belt bites into her. She rubs her flat stomach. I'm going to be a poet, a writer or I don't know what, but I'll be something, someone. She pulls off the diamond ring.